The Forgotten Horse

The Forgotten Horse

Elaine Heney

"Listening to the horse is the most important thing we can do"

Elaine Heney

First Edition Feb 2022 | Published by Grey Pony Films

www.greyponyfilms.com

Table of Contents

About Elaine Heney

Elaine Heney is an Irish horsewoman, film producer at Grey Pony Films, #1 best-selling author, and director of the award-winning 'Listening to the Horse™' documentary. She has helped over 120,000+ horse owners in 113 countries to create great relationships with their horses. Elaine's mission is to make the world a better place for the horse. She lives in Ireland with her horses Ozzie & Matilda. Find Elaine's books at **www.writtenbyelaine.com** This is the first book in the Connemara Horse Adventure Series.

Online horse training courses

Discover our series of world-renowned online groundwork, riding, training programs and iPhone and Android apps. Visit Grey Pony Films & learn more: **www.greyponyfilms.com**

Chapter 1

The little grey pony swished his tail and lifted his head, shaking off a few beads of early morning dew. He snorted, and clouds of steam erupted from his nostrils as if he were some sort of cute, fluffy dragon. The thought made Clodagh snort a giggle as she watched him through the living room window. She imagined what it might be like to ride around the field on the little grey pony. To feel the damp early morning mist on her face as they cantered up the slight incline of the field towards the old manor house. She sighed deeply, leaning her elbows on the cold windowsill and staring at the pale rising sun casting pink hues over the grass and momentarily giving the pony a peach-coloured coat.

She was so engrossed in her daydream she barely noticed the squeak of the sitting room door as it opened. The sound of shuffling feet ended with a thump as someone sat heavily down on the old floral couch she knew was behind her. Clodagh turned, hoping it was her Dad, but already knowing it wasn't. Her older brother Sam acknowledged her good morning with a grunt, never taking his eyes off the video game he was playing, but he did pop in a pair of earphones so that the beeping noise of the game abruptly stopped. Clodagh rolled her blue eyes and turned back to look at the pony again. She wondered where he'd come from? He hadn't been there last night when she'd gone to bed, and she hadn't heard anything, which seemed odd given that she could see the paddock from her bedroom window. Basil the dog nudged open the door and padded over to her, pressing himself against her side. She absently put her arm around the chocolate Labrador, pulling him into her a little. It was cold without the fire lit. Basil was warm and snuggly. He absently licked her hand and she giggled, petting his head, her eyes never lifting from the grey pony.

Clodagh bit her lip as she watched him grazing happily, then she glanced over at Sam. Slipping off the window seat, she crept over and sat down on the couch next to him, Basil trailing behind her. She looked sideways at her brother from behind her curtain of blond hair. He ignored her, continuing to tap the keys on his game. She watched as things she couldn't identify moved across the screen, blowing up in showers of colourful pixels. Finally, a big 100 crossed the centre of the screen and his fingers paused. A little smile played at his lips, and she knew whatever that 100 meant, it was a good thing.

"Sam," she said just loud enough for him to hear with his headphones on. "When did the pony come?"

"What pony?" he asked, still staring at the screen and tapping a few buttons.

"The one in the paddock out front."

"I don't know" he replied as the next level of his game began to load. "Didn't know there was a pony."

"Sam?" their mother's voice called from the kitchen, "Have you lit the fire? The guests will be up soon."

"Ugh!" Sam sighed, knocking off the game, pulling himself off the couch and straightening his black sweatshirt. "I'm never going to beat my best score."

Sam stalked off towards the fire, shoving the game into the back pocket of his black jeans as he went. Clodagh slipped off the couch and headed down the corridor towards the kitchen. Maybe Ma knew something about the pony. The smell of bacon reached her nose long before the sight of her mother did. Clodagh was sick of the smell. The B&B guests always seemed to opt for full English breakfasts, and just once she wished breakfast smelt of fresh toast and juice rather than cooked bacon, egg and coffee. She pushed open the kitchen door bracing for the smell to get stronger.

Clodagh's mother looked up from the pan and smiled when she walked in. She wiped her hands on her apron and popped some toast in the large silver toaster that sat by the window. Clodagh plopped down on one of the wooden chairs sat around the huge farmhouse kitchen table as her mother passed her some hot buttered toast on a plate and a glass of juice.

"Morning sweetie. Guest's will be up soon, once you've had your toast be a love and put some cutlery out for me, will you?"

"Sure Ma," Clodagh replied, taking a bite of the thick buttered toast. "Ma? Do you know anything about the pony?"

"Pony?" her mother asked distractedly, turning a sausage in the pan while simultaneously filling a jug for coffee.

"Yes, the grey one in the paddock out front."

"Erm," Clodagh's mother began getting plates out of one of the wooden cupboards and stacking them while checking the pans of sizzling sausage, bacon, egg and beans.

"Ma?" Clodagh said. "The pony?"

"Oh, where did I put that new box of teabags?" her mother muttered, pulling open several cupboards and a drawer Clodagh knew contained batteries and assorted knick knacks but definitely not earl grey, before finding the tea. She began filling a little basket with various types, making sure they were neatly presented.

"Ma!"

"What, sweetie?"

"Weren't you listening to me at all?" she asked, suddenly feeling invisible.

Her mother stopped and looked at her with a smile. "I'm sorry, love, you know things are tight for us at the moment. We need to get good reviews from the guests. Everything has to be perfect."

Clodagh felt bad. She knew the B&B hadn't done so well this year. Both Ma and Dad were worried about it. There was usually at least a trickle of guests throughout the year, and some months they were packed full, especially in the summer months and over Christmas, but not this year.

"I know," she nodded. "I just wanted to know about the pony."

"Yes, the pony, I'm sorry love. I don't know anything about a pony. To be honest, I didn't know there was one in the paddock at all. Your Dad's out back though. Why don't you ask him." Clodagh stuffed the last bit of toast in her mouth, feeling a little happier, and headed towards the door.

"After the cutlery!" her mother called out.

Clodagh walked out into the main hallway past the teak sideboard with its pretty inlaid flowers and glass top. Her attention flicked for a moment to the photo of Aunt Lisa on her beautiful bay horse Matilda. A frozen moment of dressage, Matilda in mid piaffe, Aunt

Lisa dressed smartly in tops and tails, her face thoughtful but smiling. Clodagh felt her heartbeat just a little faster. She wished that were her, that she could ride like Aunt Lisa. She reached out her hand, her fingers gingerly brushing the picture for a second.

"Wish you were here Aunt Lisa," she muttered.

The sounds of people moving around upstairs echoed down the huge staircase, snapping her out of the daydream. The guests were up. She glanced longingly at the front door but forced herself to go towards the dining room instead. Grabbing cutlery from the Welsh dresser that dominated the far wall of the dining room as she passed it, she set out the knives and forks as quickly as she could. The couple staying with them were just emerging from their room when Clodagh slipped back through the door to the dining room. She darted for the porch door as quickly as she could, keen not to be waylaid. The elderly couple was lovely, but she didn't want to spend the next hour chatting to them about the local historical sites when there was a pony to learn about.

As soon as she opened the front door though, she wished she'd looked for her gloves as well as her coat and wellies. There was a distinct nip to the autumn breeze that made her fingers tingle. She blew on them and then pushed them as deeply as she could into the pockets of her wax jacket. The sound of an axe hitting wood broke the quiet of the morning, and she quickly followed the sound around the side of the house to the wood store. Dad swung the axe, chopping the log in half before throwing the pieces roughly in the direction of the little wooden hut wedged behind a bush next to the big, black wrought iron gates.

"Morning peanut." he called as Clodagh ran up. "Do me a favour, put them bits in the store would you?"

Clodagh gathered up the wood and began stacking it while Dad chopped more. "Dad, do you know anything about the grey pony in the paddock?"

"No, sorry peanut, but I'm seeing Mrs. Fitzgerald this afternoon about the new fencing. I can ask her if you like."

Clodagh beamed. "Thanks, Dad."

For a few minutes, they worked quietly, with only the sound of the birds and the splitting wood to be heard. Clodagh wondered just how much wood Dad was planning on chopping, the store looked pretty full to her, but her thoughts quickly drifted back to the pony and then to Aunt Lisa. If Aunt Lisa was here, she could learn so much about horses, maybe about the pony too? Perhaps she could ride with her again.

"Dad, is Aunt Lisa coming for Christmas this year?" she asked.

"Nope, sorry peanut," Dad replied, swinging the axe again.

"Well, could we go visit her?" she asked hopefully. Visiting Aunt Lisa would be even better than her coming here since Matilda lived with her on the smallholding.

Dad paused and stood up, resting the axe on the wood stump he used for chopping. He looked at Clodagh with a smile, but his grey-blue eyes looked sad. "Christmas is a busy time, Clodagh. We need guests and the revenue this year more than ever. Maybe we can next year if business picks up."

Clodagh sighed, she knew he was right, but it didn't make it any better. Why did Aunt Lisa have to live in Ireland, so close yet so far? Dad rested the axe on the ground and stretched a little.

"Breakfast time, I think. Are you coming?"

"I've had mine," she replied. "I might just go say hi to the pony."

"Alright, don't be out all morning, though, and no going off in the woods without telling anyone." She nodded, and as soon as Dad headed back to the house, she ran towards the paddock.

Chapter 2

The yellow gravel crunched under Clodagh's wellington boots as she jogged across the driveway to the tarmac road that ran past the gatehouse up to the manor. Crossing over the road, she made her way across the grassy verge to the paddock, kicking away a few twigs that had fallen from the old apple trees dotted here and there. The little grey pony glanced up as she reached the gate, making her smile. He gave a little nicker and wandered towards her, his fluffy grey ears flicking back and forth.

"Hi," Clodagh said. He stopped a few steps away from the wooden gate, watching her with gentle, weary brown eyes. "It's ok."

Clodagh glanced around the field and noticed a large blue bucket on its side by the fence. It looked too big to be a feed bucket. Stepping back from the gate, she walked along the fence line to the bucket. The breeze blew it a little, making it roll a bit and spilling some water out. The little grey pony spooked sideways with a little jump and a snort, shaking his head. It made Clodagh giggle. He didn't really seem scared of the bucket. It was more like an excuse to have a trot about she thought.

"Did you tip this over?" she asked. He replied with a snort and a flick of his ears. "I guess this needs refilling then, huh?"

She reached out and took hold of the fence. The wood felt rough and dry under her fingertips. Carefully she began to climb over, hoping the old fence would be alright, Dad had been going on about replacing some of the fences for ages, and the paddock was the first on his list. The pony stood watching her, his ears pricked, head up high, nostrils flared.

"It's ok, don't worry," Clodagh said reassuringly. "I just need to come to get your bucket. Then I can fill it up with fresh water, ok?" She swung her leg over the fence, finding a rung on the other side to put her foot on. The old wood was slippery, and she made sure her foot was secure before swinging the other leg over and landing in the field. "See, all good." The pony looked at her, his ears still moving like little fluffy satellites. She smiled at him.

Clodagh picked up the bucket and popped it over the fence before carefully climbing back over herself. She picked up the bucket and glanced back at the pony with a smile before darting off to the outside tap. She filled the bucket as quickly as she could, the water gushing into it, splashing her a little as she did. Picking it up, she struggled towards the field as fast as she could. The bucket was too heavy to lift over the fence, so she made her way to the gate.

"Hey there," she called out as she pulled back the latch pushing he gate open just a little before heaving the bucket in.

The pony looked up and snorted at her just a little, puffs of steam erupting from his soft grey nose. Clodagh remembered what Aunt Lisa had said, stay calm, stay still, he'll come to you. She closed the gate and waited patiently by it as he walked over, eyeing the bucket. Once he was close enough, he lowered his head and began to drink the cool water. Clodagh longed to reach out her fingers and touch his coat, feel his silky mane, but she just knew somehow it would scare him. She just had to wait. She could almost hear Aunt Lisa's voice saying he'll come to you when he's ready, be patient. The pony drank until the bucket was almost empty before lifting out his head. Drips of water cascaded from his whiskers, and he licked his lips, scattering some that dribbled onto Clodagh, who laughed, brushing the droplets of water off her jacket.

"Hey! Wow, thirsty huh? You want some more?" He snorted and shook himself. "Ok, be right back."

Clodagh headed back to the tap carrying the blue bucket. She refiled it swiftly and staggered back to the paddock with it. She had expected the pony to have wandered off to graze, but he stood patiently waiting when she returned. He moved away from the gate a few steps to let her in, and she put the bucket back in place. This time he seemed less interested in the water and more interested in her. Slowly Clodagh reached out and gently brushed her fingers over the pony's neck. He flicked his ears at her, but he seemed happy enough. She eased forward and patted his neck, scratching him a little, her fingers engulfed in thick grey fur. He seemed to really enjoy it, leaning in a little. As he grew more confident and comfortable with her, he rubbed his face on her arm and shoulder.

"Itchy, are you?" she asked. She began to rub his forehead, and he relaxed, letting her pet him. "What's your name buddy? Mines Clodagh. That's my house, well it's where I live. My Mum runs the B&B, and Dad works on the manor. That's the big house right by the top of your field."

Clodagh glanced across the paddock and the one that sat empty next to it. At the far side of the field, she could clearly make out the side of the old manor, its glass conservatory glinting in the sun. The grey walls looked somehow sad and drab even in the sunshine. Even the ivy climbing the walls looked bedraggled, less green than woody and bare. Clodagh wondered if it was winter that made the place look so dreary, the neglect or if it was something else, something intangible that had stripped it of some life. The pony nudged and snuffled around at her pockets, making her pay attention to him instead.

"There's nothing in there, I'm afraid." She smiled, patting him. "But Ma might have a spare carrot in the kitchen. I'll take a look later. She'll be too busy to ask right now. We have a few people staying. It's sort of weird having strangers coming and going again. The B&B was closed for a while for renovations. Ma and Dad say it's great the guests are back, they were worried about having enough money coming in."

Clodagh climbed up onto the fence and sat on the top rung. The pony followed her, still keen for fusses and attention. "You know my aunt has a horse. Her name is Matilda. She lives in Ireland, teaching people to ride and working with troubled horses. She has her own small place too, where she has a couple of horses. I think you'd like it. I wish she lived there then she could teach me to ride more often, and I'd have someone to talk to," the pony nickered. "Other than you." Clodagh smiled. "It would be great to go visit her too, see Ireland. There are tons of amazing places to go hacking near where she lives. I'd love to go out hacking, cantering up hills." She sighed, slipping back into her daydream for a second while still scratching the pony's neck.

"One day, I'm going to work with horses too," she said, rubbing the pony's head. "Aunt Lisa taught me to ride already, but I'm going to learn more, and I'm going to do what she does. I bet it's the best job in the world. I don't think I could do what Ma does, working with people and making breakfast every day, running around cleaning up after them. Dad's job is better. At least he gets outside more. He's going to work on the fences soon. Maybe he'll do your paddock. Would you like that? Guess not. You'd probably prefer some company huh?"

Clodagh looked over the pony. Clumps of mud were all over his wide rump, making his coat stick up in places. There were a couple of grass stains on his side, and his tail looked tangled and unkempt. "Does someone come and look after you? You don't look very clean." The pony absently tossed his head. "Sorry, but it's true, you could use a brush. It looks like your owner is going to be busy getting you sorted out tonight."

"Clodagh! Dinner's ready love and come down off that fence. Dad hasn't fixed it yet." Ma called from the front door. Clodagh rolled her eyes but smiled.

"Oh, that's my Ma," she said to the pony. "Be right in." She called over her shoulder, climbing carefully down off the paddock fence.

She lent back over it, giving the little grey pony another pat and ruffling his forelock. "I guess my lunch is ready, but I'll come back and see you again. Maybe I can scrounge that carrot too." She brushed some moss from the back of her old coat and headed back towards the house.

Ma was already going back inside, pulling her cardigan closer around her. Clodagh began to walk back over the verge, glancing back at the pony who stood watching her go. He didn't leave the gateway until she was almost at the front door, and even as she began to pull her wellingtons off in the porch, he only moved a few feet away before starting to graze.

Everyone was in the kitchen sitting around the table when Clodagh came in. She went to pull out a chair, looking longingly at the large cheese toasty waiting for her on her plate.

"Er, hands, young lady," Ma said.

Clodagh sighed and walked over to the Belfast sink, turning on the large curved tap and running her hands under the warm water. It made her fingers tingle. She dried her hands on the towel hung by the sink and rushed back to her toasty. Her tummy rumbled loudly. Being outside in the cold all morning could really build an appetite. She grabbed the toasty and stuffed it in her mouth. Basil absently wandered up and sat next to her, looking up with big puppy dog eyes. Clodagh smiled at him as best she could around the toasty.

"Basil," Ma warned. He glanced at her and then turned back to Clodagh, his tongue flopping out in a doggy smile. Clodagh shrugged.

"Slow down, kid," Dad said as Clodagh took another large bite.

"Sorry," she mumbled around the cheese. "Dad, did you see Mrs. Fitz? Does she know anything about the pony?"

"Mrs. Fitz*gerald*" Ma corrected. "And don't talk with your mouth full." Clodagh fought the urge to roll her eyes.

"I asked. She said he belongs to someone who's rented the field for a month or so," Dad said from behind the paper.

"And?" Clodagh asked. "Is that it? Does he have a name? What sort of pony is he? Who owns him?"

"I have no idea what sort of pony he is, I don't know who owns him, but I think he's called Ozzie," Dad added.

"Ozzie," Clodagh repeated with a smile. It suited him.

Chapter 3

Clodagh pulled the white cotton sheet off the bed and glanced out of the window. Ozzie was standing in the middle of the paddock, seemingly enjoying the sunshine and the grass. She wished she was outside with him. She imagined it was summer, and she was lying in the soft grass filled with wildflowers enjoying the warmth while he grazed nearby.

"Clodagh, don't forget to open the window and air the room once you've stripped the bed, love," Ma called from the hallway, shattering her daydream.

Clodagh sighed. "Yes, Ma."

At least she was in the front room so she could watch Ozzie as she sorted out the bed. She finished pulling the bedding off and throwing it into the laundry basket for Ma before she went over to the window and pulled up the sash. The cool breeze made the grey tartan curtains ruffle. Ozzie glanced up for a second, and she waved at him. No one had been to visit him so far, and she wondered how long it would be before she could see who his owner was.

Picking up the basket, she headed out into the hallway. There were only two rooms left this week, and Ma had already stripped one down. She dropped the basket off with Ma and went towards the living room. She pushed open the door a crack to see Sam busy playing a video game through the TV. She paused for a moment before deciding not to go in. Sam was always annoyed when she interrupted him playing.

"Ma," she called out, suddenly having an idea. "Should I take Basil for a walk?"

Ma appeared from the kitchen. She smiled brightly. "That's nice love. Where are you going?"

"Down through the woods and back," she replied. A knowing smile spread across Ma's face.

"Alright, be careful and take the high path, stay well back off that stream and no crossing the ford. There was heavy rain last week, and I bet it's running fast."

"Ok," Clodagh said, grabbing Basil's lead and jingling it. The chocolate lab came bounding up to her, bouncing a little and wagging his tail so hard his whole body wiggled. "Come on then Basil we're off."

Basil bounced along beside Clodagh, looking up at her every now and then as if asking where they were going, was there going to be an adventure? He liked an adventure, especially if there were smells. He sniffed the breeze happily. It made Clodagh smile. They headed down the drive and over the verge to the paddock, walking along the fence line towards the woods at the far side. Ozzie looked up at them as they walked. After a few moments, he trotted over towards them, keeping an ear pointed at Basil.

"Hi, Ozzie," Clodagh said, pausing by the fence. The pony pricked his ears up at the name and then snorted at Basil as the dog put his paws on the lower rung of the fence and stared through the gap.

"This is Basil. Basil, Ozzie. Ozzie, Basil. It's ok Ozzie. No one is friendlier than Basil." She ruffled Basil's head, and he lifted his nose a bit so he could lick her hand. Ozzie seemed to decide that Basil was alright and came over to the fence for a pat too. Clodagh fussed him for a moment and then set off on her walk again. Ozzie seemed to decide that whatever they were doing was more interesting than what was happening in his field, so he'd tag along and follow them along the fence line.

At the far corner of the paddock, he stopped and watched as Clodagh and Basil headed into the woods, the bare trees partly blocking them from his view. He stood forlornly watching them, his ears pricked hopefully. Clodagh stopped and looked back at him through the branches. He looked as if he badly wanted to come with them on their walk, and she felt a little bad about leaving him behind.

"Sorry Ozzie," she said. "We'll be back in a bit."

He whickered at her hopefully, and she smiled. Basil was already trotting amongst the damp leaves, sniffing here and there, his tail wagging excitedly. Clodagh began to wander along the muddy trail that ran parallel to the paddock through the woods. In the summer it would have been impossible to see Ozzie at all from her path, but the late autumn trees, divested of their foliage, let her glimpse him from time to time through the bare branches. He stood watching the trail she and Basil had taken before trotting up the fence line and back, trying to see where they had gone. Clodagh and Basil wandered along the path. It was nice to be outside, even if it was a little chilly. Basil divided his time between darting after a good smell and checking Clodagh was still nearby while Clodagh kept her eye on Ozzie and enjoyed the fresh air.

Eventually, the trail led to a fork, one path leading up the incline towards the top paddock and the manor, the lower one down deeper into the woods beside the stream. Basil stood at the split, waiting until she caught up. Ma was right. The stream was almost overflowing, cascading rapidly over the little ford and rushing away through the woods. Clodagh called Basil away from the stream, and they headed up the path together towards the big house. It was always her favourite trail to take. The old manor was impressive, and Clodagh often found herself wondering what it had been like in the past. Today the windows paint peeled a little in places, and the old conservatory glass often had a green bloom on the panes in places. The ivy that ran up one wall seemed to suffocate the building; it was so overgrown and, in the winter, it seemed to go thin and sparse, framing a good part of one wall in gnarled stick-like branches. The garden too had seen better times. Dad did his best, keeping the grass trimmed, but the flowers were mostly gone apart from the huge rhododendrons that ran rampant and the odd holly bush that had taken over. There was an old coach store and stables at the side and back of the house. Clodagh had seen them once when she'd gone there with Dad. It had made her sad. They were full of clutter and old furniture that was covered in tarps and thick dust. It seemed wrong that such nice stone stalls didn't have ponies in them.

Clodagh and Basil reached the top of the incline. The trail sloped away again down back towards the stream, but Clodagh led Basil through the trees into the manor garden. Mrs. Fitz never minded if they cut through the gardens back to the drive, so long as they kept to the edge by the top paddock fence. Basil ran ahead, sniffing around a few of the rhododendron bushes. The pale sunlight began to fade, casting long shadows from the old manor. It was pretty spooky at times and Clodagh wondered if Mrs. Fitz ever felt creeped out living there alone with only Pip the spaniel for company.

Ozzie seemed to have spotted them and trotted to the top of his own paddock, watching as they wandered along back toward the drive. They passed through the little garden gateway into the old coach yard. The dark green double doors to the coach house were peeling, and the old yard was covered in moss. It was super slippery underfoot, and Clodagh was suddenly very pleased she had her wellingtons on. Basil sniffed happily around the old stone mounting block before she called him over to her. She didn't want him going around the corner and ending up in the back of the manor.

They reached the drive and started to walk along it. There was no real fence next to the drive, just an old deep ha-ha ditch. Ozzie had strolled over, but seemed uncertain about the ditch. He walked along with it instead keeping his eyes firmly on Clodagh. When they reached the gatehouse she cut over to the fence to say hello again.

"No one came to see you, huh?" He snorted and tossed his head. Something about him looked odd. Clodagh looked more closely. "Silly boy, where have you been?" Ozzie swished his tail, or tried to. It was knotted up with burrs and a few twigs. Clodagh climbed over the fence and carefully ran her hand down his neck, over his back and flanks. When he stood happily, she gently picked up his tail and began to untangle it, teasing out the sticky burrs and tossing them over the fence.

"There," she said once she'd finished, she gave him a scratch on his neck and a quick pat. He swished his tail as if testing it out as she climbed back over the fence to the waiting Basil. She giggled and gave him a final scratch before heading back home, the chocolate lab trailing behind her seeking out any last sniffs before bedtime.

The house phone was ringing when she closed the front door and pulled her boots off. Stepping into the hallway she realised that no one was answering it. Dad was nowhere in sight, Ma was on the B&B phone taking a booking, and Sam, as usual, was sitting playing a game with his headphones in, oblivious to the world. Clodagh sighed and walked over to the phone, picking it up.

"Hello?"

"Clodagh?" Aunt Lisa's voice filtered through the phone.

"Aunt Lisa!" Clodagh said excitedly. "How are you? How is Matilda? Oh, oh, there's a new pony here!"

"Slow down," Aunt Lisa laughed. "I'm fine, I've been teaching all morning, but I had the afternoon off so Matilda and I had a nice long hack around the lanes. It's been really sunny here today. Did you say there was a pony there?"

"Aha, his name is Ozzie. He's sort of white-grey with a few flea-bitten marks. He's so sweet Aunt Lisa, he tipped over his bucket and I filled it for him and he was rubbing his head on me and nuzzling my pocket. Then tonight he was all tangled with burrs in his tail and he let me take them out!"

"Didn't his owner do that?" Aunt Lisa asked slightly more seriously.

"I haven't seen them," Clodagh replied.

"You mean no one came at all?" Aunt Lisa asked. Clodagh could almost see her frowning on the other end of the phone.

"No," Clodagh replied.

"And he had no water?" she asked.

"No, I think he may have tipped it out. I filled his bucket for him though," Clodagh said.

"Maybe you should keep an eye on him, make sure he has water each day. I'll talk to your Dad to see if he can ask around about him."

"I will. Did you teach at the farm this morning?" Clodagh asked.

"No, I was at the client's place. It was really nice; they have a really big indoor arena and they've said I can bring Matilda by next time and ride after our lesson. You know our school is outdoor, it's not exactly fun in there in the sleet." Aunt Lisa giggled. Clodagh imagined what it would be like living on a farm with horses, spending time with other horse lovers, and riding in arenas, hacking over fields. It was like paradise even if there was sleet.

"You know," Aunt Lisa said, cutting through Clodagh's thoughts. "I think some of my old horse stuff is stored in your Dad's garage. There may be some brushes and a hoof pick in there. They might come in handy if your friend Ozzie gets himself in a tangle again."

"Really!" Clodagh said excitedly. "I could borrow them?"

"If you can find them, they're yours. They'll need a clean though," Aunt Lisa said. The sound of a dog barking in the background broke through. "Molly says hello and she needs to go out," Aunt Lisa laughed. "Tell your Dad I called and get him to ring me back when he has a few minutes ok."

"Ok," Clodagh replied.

"Oh, and Clodagh, if you need any advice or help, if that pony's owner doesn't come, just call me ok?"

"I will aunt Lisa, bye."

"Bye."

Clodagh hung up the phone and rushed across the hallway to the door that led to the garage. She knew exactly where Aunt Lisa's boxes were. She'd discovered them last summer when she'd helped Dad organize the garage. She clicked on the light and headed over to the shelving unit at the far side. Sure enough, there on the second shelf up were three boxes with Aunt Lisa's name written on the side.

She carefully pulled the boxes down. The first one was full of old riding clothes and a pair of boots. Clodagh slid it back and took the next one down. In it were an old headcollar, a few brushes, a red hoof pick, and a little wooden box. Clodagh took out the grooming things and picked up the box, running a finger over the smooth box. She carefully lifted the lid to peek inside. On top were several photographs of a girl on a pony and under them a few rosettes.

Clodagh pulled everything out reverently. First, she looked at the rosettes with their bright ribbons and boldly printed gold numbers, on the back in neat handwriting, Aunt Lisa had detailed what event they were for and a date. It made Clodagh smile, Aunt Lisa must have been around her age when she won some of them. She placed every one back in the box and turned to the pictures. Clearly, the girl was Aunt Lisa, the pony Clodagh knew was called Mystery, she had been aunt Lisa's loan pony as a child. In a few of the pictures aunt Lisa was sitting on the little black pony or stood next to her in a field, but one looked different. Here she was dressed up in showing attire and the pony had a red ribbon pinned to her bridle. There was somehow something very familiar about the picture but Clodagh couldn't figure out what. For a long time, she sat staring at the photo, taking in every detail, eventually though she put it back in the box still confused as to why the place in the photo looked so familiar.

She put the box back on the shelves and gathered up all the brushes. They smelt a little foisty and the curry comb had rusted a little, but with a good clean Clodagh thought they'd be almost as good as new. She scurried off to find Ma and ask about something to clean them with.

Chapter 4

Clodagh ran the brush over Ozzie's back. He lifted his head from the grass for a second and nuzzled at her. Thanks to daily brushes for a few days he was looking much tidier. No more mud patches, no green grass stains, and no burrs in his tail. Clodagh smiled proud of her efforts. She put the brushes back into the old cloth satchel she had hung on the fence. Ozzie followed her investigating the green bag, she gently pushed his nose out of it with a chuckle.

"Ozzie." She shook her head. "There's no food in there."

Realising there was nothing in the bag for him, Ozzie wandered over to his water bucket. He lowered his head into it and snorted a little. Then he gently tapped it with his hoof and then picked it up by the handle and threw it around a bit before tossing it onto the floor. Clodagh smiled.

"Empty huh?" she said, "Maybe I should have checked it before I got out the brushes. Give me a minute, I'll go fill it up."

Ozzie glanced at her and then began to roll the bucket around with his nose, pushing it upright and then tipping it over again. It almost reminded Clodagh of Basil with his ball. She smiled and slung the brush bag over her shoulder before picking up the empty bucket.

"You should be careful with this; I don't think your owner would bring you a new one and I'm not sure Dad has a spare one."

Clodagh gave him a pat before climbing out of the field. She dropped the brushes by the door before filling up the bucket. It was heavy when full, and Clodagh stopped a couple of times as she carried it back to the field. She had almost made it back to the paddock when she saw Mrs. Fitz walking along the fence line, her springer spaniel, Pip, scurrying along by her heels. Clodagh opened the gate and put the water in.

She was closing the gate as Mrs. Fitz walked up. Clodagh always thought it was odd that Mrs. Fitz always had her grey hair up in a bun and seemed to constantly be wearing an old green wax jacket, paisley scarf, and tweed skirt. She absently wondered if she had a whole wardrobe full of the same things or if that was all she had?

"Morning Mrs. Fitzgerald," Clodagh said, remembering not to call her Mrs. Fitz, she wasn't sure the old lady would approve, but for sure her Ma wouldn't.

"Good morning," she replied. "What were you doing in the paddock?"

Clodagh froze for a second. She swallowed hoping she wasn't about to get into trouble. "Ozzie had no water. I just refilled his bucket."

"I see," Mrs. Fitz said thoughtfully. "And those other times?"

"Other times?" Clodagh asked.

"I think I've seen you fill that bucket up for a few days now. Has he been drinking a lot?"

"I don't think so," Clodagh replied. "Just no one fills his bucket. Well, that is no one other than me."

"His owner hasn't been by?" Clodagh shook her head and Mrs. Fitz narrowed her eyes just a little. "I see," she said. She looked a little annoyed, though Clodagh got the distinct impression her irritation wasn't aimed at her. "He's a nice smart pony, he should be being ridden again. Terrible waste just being stood in a paddock. Is your father around?"

"Yeah, he's out in the back garden sorting the greenhouse for the winter," Clodagh replied. Mrs. Fitz nodded and headed off towards the garden. "Pip." The spaniel bounded after her and Clodagh let out a breath she hadn't even known she was holding. She leant back against the gate and Ozzie popped his head over it beside her watching the older lady walk away. She rubbed his velvet soft muzzle for a second.

Clodagh was cleaning the mud off her wellingtons when Mrs. Fitz left. A few minutes later Dad came around to the front of the house calling for her. Clodagh turned off the tap and rushed over to find out what he wanted, the fear that she was in trouble creeping in again.

"Yes, Dad?"

"Mrs. Fitzgerald isn't happy that the pony's owner has been neglecting him," he began. "She's going to have words with him about it, apparently he's behind in paying her too. Temporarily she wants me to take care of him, but I don't have time. Instead, I volunteered you."

"Me?" Clodagh said, surprised. Dad nodded.

"You." A smile spread over Clodagh's face. "You'll need to check on him, keep his water topped up, and make sure the paddock is safe. She is happy for you to brush him and take him for walks in the paddock, no taking him out of it." She hugged Dad and then rushed over to the paddock calling Ozzie, hardly able to contain her excitement.

The next morning, she was up early, desperate to go and see Ozzie. School was due to start next week and she was desperate to get as much time with Ozzie as possible. She had the whole day planned out - but before she could step out of the door Ma caught her.

"Clodagh, I know you have chores with Ozzie but you still need to help me sort the Halloween decorations out and carve the pumpkins."

"Ma," Clodagh almost whined. "No one is going to trick or treat. We had one kid last year."

"That was last year. It's different now. Come on, you used to love Halloween." Ma said.

"Fine," Clodagh said. "I'll sort Ozzie's water and then do it ok?"

Ma nodded. Clodagh rushed out. Ozzie was waiting by the gate, his bucket empty on the other side of the fence. He pointed an ear at it as if saying 'look I put it there for you'. He pawed the ground near the bucket to emphasise his point. Clodagh smiled and gave him a fuss before filling the bucket.

"I promise I'll be done as fast as I can, then we can have a brush."

She rushed back to the house where Ma had left out the Halloween decorations. Everything had a usual place so it wouldn't take too long to put out. Ozzie watched her from the gateway while she hung up the garlands of bat shapes and put out a few pumpkins that lit up along the driveway. He seemed interested in what she was doing and what the odd orange balls with eyes were. It took almost the whole morning for her to do and Clodagh felt more and more frustrated, but Ozzie was enjoying it immensely. It was very entertaining watching the nice blonde girl putting out the silly looking things.

Finally, after lunch she was free. She ran to the paddock, the brush bag bouncing by her side. Ozzie had wandered off to the middle of the field and was happily munching on the grass. She decided to take all her chores seriously. She glanced over checking his water was full as she climbed the fence. Since it was, she began to walk the fence, checking the paddock for any issues. She hadn't gone far when the sound of hoofbeats heralded the approach of Ozzie. He trotted to her and fell in step beside her. Absently she reached over scratching his neck. Together they followed the fence line. Sometimes he'd pause and eat a little before trotting to catch up. Sure that the paddock was sound Clodagh led the way back to the gate.

Clodagh pulled Aunt Lisa's old headcollar out of the brush back. It fitted Ozzie like a glove and made her smile. It wasn't like she really needed it, but somehow having it fit felt reassuring. She left the halter on for a bit, unclipping the lead rope and putting it on the fence. Grabbing the brushes, she began to groom Ozzie, cleaning away mud and green grass stains, pulling a comb through his mane and tail, and scratching any itchy spots she found. Ozzie almost began to doze as Clodagh worked away. His lower lip began to flop and he rested his back foot, calmly enjoying the pampering and the sunshine on his back.

The sun was beginning to sink a little when Clodagh finally finished cleaning Ozzie. His tail and mane were silky smooth and he almost shone in the fading light. She climbed on the fence to enjoy the view. The sunlight made everything look slightly golden. Ozzie sidled up to the fence, hoping for more scratches. Without a thought, she reached out and started scratching his neck just by his withers. It made his nose twitch and he wiggled it back and forth a bit.

Clodagh smiled. "That's the spot, is it?"

Clodagh looked over the paddock. She wondered what it would be like to ride Ozzie around the paddock. Mrs Fitz had said he had been ridden before, Oh how wonderful would it feel to walk by the woods, to trot up the incline towards the manor. Without thinking she stood a little on the fence. He was so close. Pausing in her scratches she took hold of some of his mane and gently slid onto his back. For a second, he seemed to tense, but she steadied her breathing and scratched his neck a little and he relaxed again. Remembering everything Aunt Lisa had taught her she took a deep breath, gathered her energy, and thought forward, putting the tiniest pressure on his side. Ozzie began walking. They were riding together. Clodagh smiled, feeling the slight breeze ruffle her hair as they went. She looked away across the paddock slightly shifting her seat as she did and Ozzie turned, following the direction she had suggested. They walked together up the incline of the paddock, past the old pear tree that grew to one side of the field near the woods, and again turned together walking along the fence.

They were parallel to the manor house now. Somehow it looked so much better from on Ozzie as if it had a magic presence that was old and faded but not dead, a spark that had been lit by them riding together as one. Clodagh breathed out, shifting her seat a little, thinking how nice it would be to pause and take in the scene. Ozzie stopped. They stood together in silence as the sun dipped lower in the sky casting a golden hue over the manor and glinting off the conservatory. In the dim light the faded, peeling paint was hidden and Clodagh felt like she had, for a moment, gone back in time. Like she was seeing the manor as it once was. A sudden realisation hit her. This was the background of Aunt Lisa's photo. The show she had won the rosette at was here, in this field. Ozzie cleared his nose and she scratched his neck.

"Home?" she suggested. They walked together back down the paddock to the gate. Clodagh reluctantly slid off his back and hung onto his neck for just a moment. He seemed to enjoy the hug and put his head over her shoulder pulling her in a little more. She scratched his withers and he wiggled his nose against her back. It had to be the most magical Halloween she'd ever had. She smiled snuggling into him. It was official. She had fallen head over heels for the pony in the paddock.

Pulling back, she took off the head collar and put it in the bag with the brushes before giving him another quick pat. She headed back to the house with a smile on her face. Ma was filling a bowl with candy when she came inside.

"Alright love?" she asked. Clodagh just nodded. "You know if you're going to walk that pony around the field you should wear a hat."

Clodagh froze worried Ma was going to tell her off, but she smiled and Clodagh let out her breath. "I know Mrs. Fitzgerald said you could exercise him a little, but safety first. Put a lead rope on that halter and a hat. Now I know you say we won't get any trick or treaters, but go put on your witch's hat and that black skirt, just in case."

"Ok, Ma." Clodagh smiled. She ran upstairs to her room, grabbing her old black skirt and a fake witch's hat from her closet and throwing them on the chair next to the old writing desk that doubled as her dressing table. She rushed over to the window. There was enough light to see Ozzie grazing happily in the field. Clodagh threw the cushions off the window seat and pulled up the lid. She pulled out a drawstring bag and opened it up. Inside was her riding hat. Aunt Lisa had bought it for her last Christmas when they had hoped she'd be able to come to visit. Unfortunately she couldn't make it, but at least now she could use the hat.

Clodagh was right, there were no trick or treaters, but Halloween was still one of the best days of the year. Riding Ozzie had been amazing and it only got better. For the rest of the half-term week, she spent time grooming him, caring for him, and riding around the paddock. As promised, she wore her hat, but she almost never put the lead rope on. Most of the time she didn't even use the head collar. They walked the field, trotted around in circles on the flat level bit at the bottom of the paddock, and even had a couple of canters up the incline. That was the most magical. The feeling of cantering along on Ozzie, the speed, the wind pulling her hair back, nothing had ever felt so right or so special. She felt completely free. She told Ozzie everything, it was so nice, she wasn't even worried about school starting. The idea of being able to come home after a day in that place and unload all of the things that had happened to a friendly listening ear was amazing. This year, this year was going to be better.

Chapter 5

The early morning sun began to filter through Clodagh's bedroom window. She yawned and stretched her arms. She turned over to look at the faint light seeping around the edges of the bedroom curtains. Two more days and she'd be back at school, but for the first time in forever that thought didn't leave her with a knot in her stomach. Now she had Ozzie to talk to and even just cantering around in the small paddock she felt free like somehow everything would be alright. She could do anything, go anywhere. Clodagh smiled, turning over and snuggling into her pillow for five more minutes.

She was imagining herself and Ozzie galloping down a sandy beach in the sun, waves breaking on the perfectly golden shore, when the odd sound of a large engine broke her thoughts. She sat up frowning. The only thing that sounded like that was the bin lorry and that certainly didn't come on a Saturday. Dad had been suggesting for a while that the manor could do with a small tractor, but there never seemed to be any money for one. Clodagh hopped out of bed to look. Maybe Mrs. Fitz had bought one. It would be just like Dad to keep it a secret and surprise everyone by turning up on it. The thought made her smile. Clodagh pulled on her thick blue jumper as she wandered over to the curtains pulling them aside to peek. As her fingers closed around the soft velvet fabric a noise made her heart skip a beat and her blood run cold. Ozzie was shouting and not in his usual happy way. He sounded panicked and afraid.

Clodagh tore back the drapes quickly and stood frozen in horror. Down below, taking up most of the driveway, was an old metal cattle truck. The sun glinted off the cold metal ramp that had been lowered ready for its recipient. A slight scattering of straw poked out of the back of the waiting wagon. A man held Ozzie on a lead rope, tugging him towards the idling truck. The little grey pony tugged back, his eyes rolling towards the field he so desperately wanted to go back to. He danced sideways and hopped a little off his front legs, his head high and neck stiffened. The man merely growled at him and tapped him across the chest with a spare bit of rope, making Ozzie pull back further, his back legs almost sliding under his front.

Without a second thought, Clodagh turned and ran for the door. She had to save Ozzie. Who was this strange man? Surely, he couldn't just turn up and take him. Where was his owner? Clodagh had secretly imagined Ozzie had a nice owner. Maybe some other girl who hadn't been able to come to see him for a really good reason. She imagined that one day the girl would turn up having broken an arm or something and say how sorry she was that she hadn't been there for Ozzie. They'd become friends and both love him. She'd have two new friends. That was a dream though and what was happening outside was very real.

Clodagh flew down the main staircase brushing past Sam who seemed to try and stop her. Tears began to form in her eyes as she thought about how scared Ozzie looked. She could only think he was longing for the nice girl who he trotted around the field with to come and save him. She would, she was coming, hold on Ozzie. Clodagh rushed past Ma and into the porch only pausing briefly to grab her boots. She flung open the door to see a grey flank passing into the back of the wagon. Dad caught hold of her, shaking her shoulders gently, making her turn away from the sight of Ozzie being loaded into the truck. He crouched down in front of her, sadness filling his blue eyes. He shook his head.

"Dad, what's happening? Who is that man? Where is Ozzie going?" she asked in a rush. She knew she was talking, but her mind felt pulled in a million directions as if she were trapped in some awful nightmare and was watching what unfolded from somewhere else. Part of her willed herself to wake up, but at the same time, she knew this was real.

"I'm so sorry sweetie," Dad said. "That's Ozzie's owner. He's come to take him to his new home."

"New home?" Clodagh said. This was his home.

Dad nodded. "He's been sold."

Sold. The word echoed around her head. She wanted to scream and shout and demand that she could buy him, but she knew that even with the entire contents of her money box she would never be able to afford him. She fought back her tears. If this, was it, if Ozzie was going, she wanted two things? To say goodbye and to find out he was going to be alright.

She straightened herself up and strode across the gravel towards the wagon. Her feet crunching the gravel. A light breeze blew through her tangled mess of blond hair and cut through the thin material of her pajama bottoms, but she didn't care. She barely noticed. She felt almost numb. As she reached the box the man who owned Ozzie was just closing a latch on the back of the ramp. The box shook as Ozzie stomped around in it and he smacked the side with his hand.

"Stop that," he said gruffly.

All daydreams of Ozzie's owner were shattered. The man was much older, probably even older than dad. He wore a flat cap from which strands of greying hair poked at odd angles. He wore typical farming clothes, his hands looked rough and chapped and his face weathered. Clodagh had seen a lot of older farmers like him before in the pub when Ma and Dad had taken them out on a Sunday sometimes for lunch, but this man looked somehow harder than they had. The man turned and looked at Clodagh, he tried to smile but it didn't reach his grey eyes that remained unwaveringly cold.

"You're Ozzie's owner." It was a statement rather than a question.

"Was my daughter's when she was interested in horses," he replied. "Couldn't keep it. She's not into horses no more and I retired. Sold up the farm."

"Where is he going?" she asked, swallowing hard, almost not wanting to know the answer.

"Riding school down the ways a bit. Don't know why they couldn't come to fetch him from the field. No, made me come get him in the truck. Flaming thing don't like it, he always was a pain to move anywhere." Clodagh fought the urge to tell the man he wasn't a pain, he was scared. The riding school. That wasn't too far away, on the way to school in fact if they cut across the manor fields. She'd still be able to see him. The thought lifted her just a little, a tiny sliver of salvation.

"Can I, can I say goodbye?" Clodagh asked.

"I ain't taking the back down, but there's holes in the side," the man said.

The cattle truck had slits in it all the way along its side. Clodagh peered through two of them before she could see Ozzie well enough. She pushed her fingers through the hole and he nuzzled at them.

"I'm sorry Ozzie," she said, tears spilling down her cheeks. "I'm sorry I couldn't stop this, that I couldn't save you. I want you, I do. It's not my choice. I swear." She hoped he understood what she was saying. She worried that he thought she didn't want him anymore, that she was sending him away. The thought broke her heart and she swallowed a sob.

The man climbed into the cab of the truck and Clodagh stepped back, straining to see Ozzie. He had calmed when she was there, but as soon as her fingers left the gap he started stomping again and shouting, calling after her. Clodagh's tears fell thick and fast. She tried desperately not to start sobbing right there in the middle of the drive. The truck began to move forwards, rolling towards the iron gateways, taking Ozzie with it. Clodagh stood frozen as the lorry pulled through the gate, past the stone pillars, and turned onto the road.

As soon as it was out of sight Clodagh was running. Running past Dad, passed Ma and Sam, ignoring everything they said. Every thought of comfort was somehow wrong. The world, her world, was ending, shattered into pieces by a farmer and a cattle truck. She heard the sound of her bedroom door slamming shut and only vaguely realised it was her that had done it. She threw herself onto her bed grabbing the pillow and let out all the tears that had been threatening to flow. She sobbed so hard she felt she could hardly catch her breath.

The bedroom door opened, but it wasn't Ma, or Dad, or Sam who came in. They knew she needed some time. It was Basil who jumped up onto the bed and laid down next to her. He put a doggy paw on her and panted. He nudged his way under her arm and licked at her salty tears. She wrapped an arm around him and pulled him close to her like a doggy lifebuoy. Downstairs she could hear Dad doing his chores, the smell of Ma making breakfast like normal wafted into her room.

"How is the world still going?" she asked Basil. "It should have stopped." He licked her face and she buried her head in his soft brown fur letting her tears fall again. Her world had just broken into pieces and yet everyone else's seemed to keep going. She almost felt like she was suffocating, like she couldn't breathe it hurt so much. She gave in and sobbed until she couldn't cry anymore.

When she did come downstairs later, Ma suggested that she help out like normal. Get back into a routine. Clodagh couldn't have disagreed more. She didn't want to go back to her old routine, it seemed like she had been living in black and white and suddenly seen in colour but was being asked to go back to dullness and grey. Still she found herself stripping the beds. Whenever she caught sight of the window though her heart felt heavy. She knew if she looked out there would be no Ozzie looking back. No grey shape eating in the distance. She folded the sheets and stuffed them in the basket. Basil sat beside her, watching expectantly. He was the only one who seemed to understand.

"Walk?" she asked.

He shot up and wagged his tail. "Woof."

They wandered down to the kitchen and Clodagh pushed the basket onto the table. Ma smiled at her, but she couldn't smile back. It felt wrong to smile, she wondered if she'd ever do it again.

"We're going for a walk," she said, her voice sounding miserable even to her.

"Good idea love, get some fresh air," Ma replied with a smile. Clodagh knew her mother was fighting hard not to run around the table and hug her. She appreciated that she didn't. She'd cried so much already she needed a break, and if Ma hugged her she knew the tears would come all over again.

Clodagh nodded and grabbed Basil's lead. They headed to the porch, passing Sam who was, as always, occupied with one of his video games. He pushed a button on his phone with a beep and looked up at her, his dark eyes filled with pity.

"Sorry about the pony," he muttered.

She swallowed hard. "Thanks." She replied not knowing what else to do and he walked away into the lounge.

Outside was better, but still felt wrong. Clodagh and Basil walked the fence line to the woods. Basil kept stopping and looking around. The big funny-looking whiteish dog that had come with them on walks lately was missing.

"You miss him too huh buddy?" Clodagh said.

"Woof."

They slipped into the shade of the woods. It had always been Clodagh's safe space, a place to reflect on things, to feel comfortable and peaceful, even on cold days. Today it seemed hollow but still better than anywhere else. She wandered amongst the trees, sometimes reaching out and touching the rough bark just to make sure things were real and she could still feel them. Basil scouted ahead, but she noticed not nearly as far as normal. He knew the girl pack member needed someone and that someone was going to be him.

They walked in melancholy silence through the woods. Clodagh couldn't help but think what Ozzie was doing. Was he in a paddock? In a warm stable maybe with a nice feed? She pictured him happily eating hay from a net surrounded by a deeply comfortable bed, but then her mind flicked back to him being roughly loaded, to that last moment her fingers brushed his velvet nose and the dream vanished.

When they walked through the manor gardens, she felt the sparkle of the old house had dimmed too. Riding Ozzie, seeing it from on him, it had flared into life for a second, like a fire whose embers had been fanned by the wind, now though it was fading back to a smolder. The peeling paint and drab grey stone made the whole house look like she felt. Mrs. Fitz was in the conservatory reading the newspaper, her reading glasses perched precariously on the end of her nose. She glanced up seeing Clodagh and Basil and nodded her usual greeting. Clodagh would normally wave back, but she could barely muster raising her hand in acknowledgment.

They passed through the rhododendrons and into the old coach yard. Clodagh looked over the old ached green doors, almost able to see the ghosts of the coach and horses ready to be bedded down for the night. She'd felt like that before, but this time all the horses looked like Ozzie and her heart hurt.

Basil walked back at her heel and whined a little. She patted his head, glad she still had a friend. It was starting to get dark and the night promised to be a cold one, she could already see her breath. She took her boots off in the porch and pushed open the door. The fire must have been lit because a wave of heat washed over her as she opened the main door, making her hands and face tingle. Usually, she loved that feeling, but not tonight. She closed the door and went straight to her room. Ma would call her for tea soon but she wasn't hungry at all.

She swung her door open and stepped inside, flicking on the light. There was something on her bed. A piece of paper lay face down on the checky duvet. She picked it up and turned it over. There was a photo of her sitting cantering on Ozzie up the incline. His mane and her hair fanned out behind them, frozen in place. Ozzie's ears were pricked and she had a huge smile on her face, they looked so happy, so perfect. Fresh tears pricked her eyes. How?

"Took it on my phone," Sam said from the doorway. She turned around to look at him leaning against the frame. He shook his dark hair out of his eyes. "Dad said I could print it out."

"Thank you," she said her eyes brimming. She hugged the photo to her as if it were more precious than all the emeralds in the world. Sam shrugged and slunk off leaving her to look at the picture. She took a frame off the desk. It had an old school photo in it. She pulled the picture out, tossing it into a drawer, putting Ozzie in its place instead. Clearing a little space on her nightstand she placed it down carefully with a sad smile. She lay down on the bed for a second staring at the photo of Ozzie.

She was sat on her bed attempting to read a book and failing when Dad came in holding his laptop. Clodagh looked up and Dad swung the computer around to reveal Aunt Lisa. Despite everything, Clodagh managed a slight smile.

"How are you doing?" she asked.

Clodagh glanced away and bit her lip so she didn't cry again, digging her fingers into her palms for good measure. Dad put the laptop down on the end of the bed and backed away to the door.

"I'll let you chat," he said with a smile.

Once he'd closed the door, Clodagh pulled the laptop closer. "Dad told you?"

"A bit," Aunt Lisa replied. "He said Ozzie's owner showed up, that he's been sold."

"It was awful," Clodagh sniffed. "He was so rough and Ozzie didn't want to go."

"I'm sorry."

"Why did he have to sell him?" Clodagh asked knowing Aunt Lisa wouldn't know the answer.

"I know, but sometimes people come into our lives for just a little while. We don't like it when they have to leave, but at least while they're there it makes things so much better. Besides, maybe Ozzie will have a nice new home now huh? Someone like you might be brushing him right now."

"But it isn't me," Clodagh grumped. "And he doesn't have a someone. The man said he went to a riding school."

"Well then at least he'll be well cared for. Most riding schools take very good care of their ponies Clodagh. Besides if it isn't far away maybe you could go ride sometimes," Aunt Lisa said.

Clodagh looked up. That thought hadn't occurred to her. The riding school was so close she could walk. She passed it on the way to school if she cut through the fields. Why couldn't she take lessons? Maybe she'd have to do extra work around the house, but she could do that.

"It's really close!" she said brightly. "The man, he said Ozzie was going to the school near here. I think it's called..."

"Briary." Aunt Lisa replied flatly. A dark look crossed her face. It made Clodagh falter, something was wrong. Clodagh got a sinking feeling in the pit of her stomach.

"Aunt Lisa?" she asked, not sure she wanted to know what her aunt was thinking.

Aunt Lisa took a deep breath. "I'm sorry, when I was young, learning to ride, Briary had a bad reputation amongst us. It was full of snooty well-to-do sorts that cared more about their jodhpurs than their horses." She paused and then smiled. "It's probably not like that now. I bet it's changed a lot. I mean the little place I learnt to ride isn't even open anymore and I can't imagine the lady that ran Briary back then does so now. It's silly."

Clodagh suddenly felt unsure. On one hand, she had hope that maybe, just maybe she'd be able to ride Ozzie again. On the other, what if the school hadn't changed. She'd never really been to Briary, just patted a few odd ponies over the fence when she'd passed by on her way to school. An uneasy feeling settled in the pit of her stomach. She was going to have to go see for herself, even if that only meant checking on Ozzie on her way to school.

"Would you mind passing me back to your Dad for a bit?" Aunt Lisa asked with a smile.

Clodagh nodded and called Dad to get the computer. She didn't mind not talking anymore, not so much because she was so down, but because she wanted to check how much was left in her money box. Maybe she had enough for a couple of lessons. The thought cheered her up no end.

She grabbed the little porcelain pony off her bookshelf. It had been a present from Aunt Lisa for her birthday. There was a little slit in the saddle for coins and notes to go in and a bung under its bay tummy to empty it out. Clodagh said it reminded her of Matilda and so she had nicknamed it her Tilly box.

"Ok, Tilly," she said pulling out the bung and shaking the money out onto the bed. "Let's see how much I have."

Chapter 6

Clodagh awoke feeling down. The money in her Tilly moneybox hadn't amounted to much. Worse still she faced the fact that tomorrow school started again and she was going to have to go, without Ozzie to come home too. She sighed and turned over pulling her blankets over her head and wishing yesterday had been a dream. A soft knocking at the door made her stir. Ma opened the door a crack and poked her head in.

"You awake love?" she asked.

For a second, she thought about pretending to be asleep, but she couldn't lie to Ma like that. "Yeah," she replied, it sounding muffled from under the duvet.

She felt the bed sink a little at the bottom and knew Ma had come in and sat down. She sat up, pushing her hair out of her face and hoping Ma would make it quick so she could go back to wallowing in her bed.

"How are you doing?" Clodagh didn't say anything. She didn't think she could without crying. She shook her head avoiding looking up. "That good huh? Well, maybe I can cheer you up."

"I doubt it," Clodagh said glumly.

"What if I told you that you could see Ozzie?"

Clodagh looked up with surprise, Ma was smiling. "You mean just go down and see how he settled? You'd take me?"

"Better than that." Ma said. "Aunt Lisa called back after you went to bed. She's arranged for you to have a lesson at Briary today at 11.00. You can go and see Ozzie and maybe if we explain everything, they'll let you ride him. Aunt Lisa said that schools normally let ponies settle in for a while before they take part in any lessons, but this is an odd situation. But if they won't let you then you can still have a lesson on one of the other ponies and see he's ok."

"Thank you," she said and she flung her arms around Ma.

"You should thank your Aunt Lisa." Ma said, she glanced at her watch. "But maybe later, you need to get some breakfast and get ready."

Clodagh never thought she'd eaten breakfast so fast in her entire life. She found her old blue jodhpurs, they were a bit faded, but at least they fit. She glanced out of the window at the frosty morning and pulled on a thick jumper Ma had knitted her, before running down to the porch and grabbing her warm waterproof coat. She eyed up her wellies. They weren't exactly good for riding in. It was fine bareback, there were no stirrups to get stuck in, but she was positive a riding school would use saddles. Ma had said it would be ok, but Clodagh wasn't sure. Then she had an idea, she grabbed the phone in the hall and quickly dialled Aunt Lisa's number.

"Hello?"

"Aunt Lisa, it's me, thank you, thank you so much for the lesson" she gushed.

"You're more than welcome Clodagh. You just go check on that pony," Aunt Lisa replied.

"Aunt Lisa, could I ask another favour?" Clodagh asked, she felt bad asking for more, but this was Aunt Lisa and the favour wasn't that big.

"Sure," her aunt replied.

"Could I borrow your old boots? I only have my wellies and I saw them the other day, I think they might be a bit big but ok if I wear my thicker socks."

"If they fit Clodagh they're yours," Aunt Lisa said. "To be honest I forgot I even had them and they would certainly be safer to ride in than your wellies."

"Thank you!" Clodagh beamed. The day was getting better and better.

"Have fun sweetie, I have to go, I have a lesson as well." She chuckled.

They hung up and Clodagh rushed into the garage and pulled out the short boots she'd found a few days before. The elastic panels on the side were a little saggy and the toes were a tad scuffed, but when Clodagh pulled them on over her thick socks they fitted pretty well. She pulled them off and carried them into the kitchen to find the black shoe polish and cleaning cloths. She polished them until they shone. She felt so proud pulling them on. She looked at herself in the hall mirror and felt like a real rider, a broad smile spread across her face.

"Well don't you look smart?" said Ma coming into the hallway, rubbing her hands on her apron. Clodagh smiled. "You certainly can't walk there in those nice shiny boots. I'll get my coat and we'll drive down."

It was only a short drive to Briary but it seemed to take forever. Clodagh felt as if she had butterflies in her stomach. She was so excited. As they pulled into the riding school car park, she couldn't help but notice the other cars. Ma's old estate car was very practical, but it looked outclassed by the big SUVs and 4 wheel drives it was parked amongst. For the first time, Clodagh felt nervous as well as excited, but this was for Ozzie.

"You want me to come with you love?" Ma asked.

"No, it's ok," she said.

"Well, I think I'll wait anyway. Might just read the paper," she said with a smile.

Clodagh smiled. She took a deep breath and stepped out of the car. The cold air hit her cheeks and she was glad to walk from the shady car park into the sun.

Clodagh walked through a pair of double gates into the school's yard. It was laid out in a 'U' shape with pristine wooden stables, each one with a clean window pulled open. There wasn't a hint of hay or bedding anywhere. It was spotless. There seemed to be two menages one to either side of the stables both being used for lessons.

She wandered over to the fence next to the smaller arena. It was filled with a group of girls, all very neatly dressed, who seemed to be doing dressage. Clodagh watched for a while, the girls all seemed to be excellent riders, but she was shocked to see most of them carried a crop. Aunt Lisa only had one client who rode with a stick. She was an older lady with a weak leg. Clodagh had met her once on a visit. She had been really nice as had her big dun horse. Clodagh remembered she had a long thin schooling stick with a little tuft on the end that she used to tap behind her bad leg sometimes when she struggled to 'communicate' with the dun as Aunt Lisa had put it. These girls didn't look like they had that problem though.

She turned her attention to the other lesson going on. Clodagh couldn't see much. The larger of the two menages was mostly hidden behind the stables and a tall fence. She could only see a single black pony cantering around and jumping a small cross pole. She noticed a few ponies in the stables though, maybe one was Ozzie. She turned her attention to the yard.

Clodagh stepped up to the first box and peered in. The stall was empty, but it had a neat, clean bed of shavings in it with rubber matting at the front. There was a large hay net and a full bucket of water. Clodagh felt herself begin to relax. It seemed nice. Maybe Ozzie would be ok here and he was close by. She could maybe come and ride. She walked up the stables past a few more empty boxes before she came face to face with a little bay. He had a cheeky-looking face with a little bit of a dish and a big bushy mane. A white stripe ran down from his forehead to his pink nose.

"Hello," Clodagh said, she reached out to pat him and he pulled back, the white of his eye showing. "Sorry, did I scare you?"

She held out her hand palm up. The pony carefully came back and sniffed her fingers a little. He regarded Clodagh sceptically before going to his hay net. Clodagh walked on. She wondered why the bay was so shy. Maybe he had been bought like Ozzie had and came from somewhere not so nice. There was a chestnut dozing over the door in the next stable. She didn't seem to notice Clodagh at all, not when she patted her, not when she spoke, not even when she gave her a scratch. Her eyes looked dull and numb. Clodagh was starting to get a bad feeling. One skittish horse was nothing, one skittish horse and one looking numb wasn't a good sign.

The dressage class seemed to end and suddenly the stables sprang to life. The girls came out leading their horses. They were chatting together ignoring both their horses and Clodagh.

"I am so going to need spurs to get her to move," one was moaning as she dragged a chestnut mare into a stable.

"Can't compete in them though," said another, leading a large grey.

"True, but it'd at least move here," the first moaned. Clodagh frowned. Had the girl really referred to her horse as 'it'?

Still, Clodagh wondered if one of the girls could tell her what she needed to do. She wasn't sure if she was supposed to tell someone she was here or wait around for someone to arrive. Aunt Lisa was the only one who had taught her before. She'd never really been to a riding school before. She stepped up to the girl with the grey.

"Excuse me." The girl looked her up and down slightly distastefully, her eyes lingering on her faded jodhpurs and old boots.

"Yes?" Clodagh swallowed, looking at the girl in her immaculate beige jodhpurs, expensive-looking boots, and new looking padded blue gilet.

"I'm booked in to have a lesson. Do I just wait here or do I need to find the instructor?"

"Newbie." The girl smiled, glancing at the other girls. "Just wait over by the fence there." She pointed to a small section of fence line just outside the big gates Clodagh had come through. "You can see how real riders have a lesson. When they're done Clair will fetch you."

"Thanks," Clodagh said politely. She wandered away to the fence, happy to be away from the girls. She heard them giggling as she left and tried to imagine they weren't chuckling about her.

Clodagh wondered where Ozzie was. She knew the riding school had four big fields and a couple of paddocks behind it they used for grazing because she walked past them to school on nice days. They belonged to Mrs. Fitz but were on the other side of the road to the manor. There was a walk all around the edge of them, Mrs. Fitz used it to walk Pip, and Clodagh and Sam used it to cut through to school. Maybe Ozzie was in one of them relaxing. She could see the paddocks were empty but the fields were out of view. Maybe after her lesson she'd walk home, Ma wouldn't mind and although it was cold, the sun was bright.

She pulled the main gate closed behind her and headed over to the fence to watch the lesson, waving at Ma as she went. She lent on the fence and froze. There was Ozzie. He stood in a line next to five other horses with an older looking boy sat on him. How was he in a lesson? Aunt Lisa had said they would let him settle in! The little black pony she'd seen before pulled back in at the end of the line and a girl on a bay took her turn to trot around the school. The pony seemed very reluctant to move and the girl kept kicking it until it trotted. She bounced about doing rising trot and didn't look stable at all in the saddle. Clodagh felt bad for the pony but not as bad as she did when it pulled up and it was Ozzie's turn.

The boy yanked at the reins to turn him, kicking him hard. Clodagh wanted to yell at him but her words wouldn't come out. She felt frozen. She watched with a sickening feeling as Ozzie trotted around, he was hollowing his back and Clodagh just knew the saddle they had put on him wasn't right. The boy though didn't seem to notice or care, he kicked to make Ozzie go faster and he seemed to thump down hard in the saddle as he went. Ozzie's eyes rolled a little, his ears pinned back flat to his neck, tail swishing. How was the boy so oblivious? When they had taken their turn the boy yanked at the reins again, pulling Ozzie back into the line and jabbing him in the mouth when he asked him to stop. Clodagh felt her heart breaking all over again. Why wasn't the instructor telling him to be gentler? To squeeze, not kick, to use their seat and gently use the reins to communicate rather than tug and pull?

The lady teaching the class she presumed was Clair seemed indifferent to her pupils and the ponies. She put up a small cross pole fence as the last pony did its circle. When it was back in line, she pointed to the first pony.

"This time trot your circle, take the fence and return to the line."

The ponies took their turns. Most of them seemed reluctant or did what they were told with a dull, distanced look barely clearing the pole. Clodagh clutched the fence so hard that her fingers were going white. Ozzie headed out to the track, the boy booted him into a trot and he tensely jogged around the school. He was starting to hold his neck high and stiffly. They headed towards the cross pole and Clodagh could see a mile off that Ozzie was not only uncomfortable but that he was backing off, he didn't have the impulsion to take the jump. He stopped in front of the poles lowering his neck as he did so and depositing the boy unceremoniously onto the poles.

The boy stood up yelling and shouting, stomping his feet like a kid having a temper tantrum. His face went beetroot red as he screamed at Ozzie. Almost immediately a woman opened the door to a black SUV near Clodagh and stormed out yelling at the instructor to 'teach that stupid pony a lesson'. Clodagh couldn't believe it. Ozzie, spooked by the fall, started to run around blindly, his reins flapping, Clodagh wanted to jump the fence and go to him, but everything seemed to move too fast.

She opened her mouth. "But, the saddle is wrong," she said, her voice lost under the screaming woman and boys yelling.

Ozzie seemed to see her for the first time, he shouted and headed for her. The instructor stopped Ozzie before he reached Clodagh, but instead of calming him down, and to Clodagh's horror, she slapped him hard on the nose and yelled at him. Ozzie pulled back away from her and she yanked at the reins, slapping his chest with a crop. He tried to pull back again, coming up a little at the front, desperate to be away from her and she growled at him. Clodagh began to feel tears form in her eyes.

"Ozzie," she shouted; she began to climb the fence determined to help him somehow, just to make the woman stop. She wanted to rip the reins away from her, to lead Ozzie out of there back home. A small part of her wanted to throw the crop at the boy too.

Her foot reached the second rung of the fence before a hand closed around her arm and gently pulled her back. She turned around to see Ma. She looked very unhappy. In fact she couldn't remember the last time she'd seen Ma so angry. Apparently, she had seen what had happened too. Clodagh looked back at Ozzie, tears already spilling down her cheeks. Ma pulled her into a hug.

"Come on love," she said amply loud enough for everyone to hear, even the snotty girls in the yard. "You can't learn anything here. People like these aren't capable of making *you* a better rider."

Her words should have made Clodagh feel better, but she felt awful. She was leaving and Ozzie wasn't. All hope of him having a wonderful life was in tatters, Briary was what her Nan used to call all fur coat and no knickers. It looked nice but there was nothing underneath. The people were snooty, the instructors mean, and the ponies, although given what they needed to live, were neglected. They were numb. Clodagh slid into the passenger side and Ma walked, head held high to her door, and got in slamming it closed.

"I'm so sorry love," she said starting the engine. "I wish there was more we could do."

Clodagh sat silently looking out from under her hair. There had to be something she could do. She was Ozzie's friend, maybe his only hope. She had to do something. She had to find a way to save him. A new grim determination settled over her. Whatever it took she wasn't going to let him stay in that horrible place.

Chapter 7

Clodagh walked along the school corridor, oblivious to everything around her. Someone brushed past her knocking her shoulder and she vaguely noticed them say 'watch it'. Her mind constantly tried to find a way to help Ozzie and failed. She'd even found herself wondering if she could somehow run away with him, hide him in the woods, but she knew that was far from realistic. The girls she hung around with at school were clustered together by the classroom door. She sidled up to them and leaned against the grey wall, clutching her old purple lever arch file to her chest.

"Hey Clodagh, did you have a nice break?" Eve asked, pushing her golden hair off her shoulders and smiling brightly. "I did, we went on holiday to Spain, oh my goodness, it was like so hot!"

"It was ok," Clodagh replied, trying to make sure her voice didn't crack. She wondered if it would make any difference if it did. Eve was nice but she was so bubbly and so focused on her own life she didn't really catch on to other people's feelings very easily.

"It's true. We went to Spain. My Dad totally burnt his shoulders," Melissa was saying. Clodagh sighed, same old same old, she could tell both of them about Ozzie and none of it would sink in at all. Neither liked horses much.

"Hey." Mike threw himself against the wall next to her. He looked as unhappy as she was.

"Hey," she replied.

"Tweedle-dee and tweedled blond still talking about how hot Spain is?" he asked, shrugging his old rucksack further onto his shoulder and nodding his head towards the girls. Clodagh nodded. "Geese, that's all I heard on the bus. Give it a rest." He ran a hand through his brown hair in frustration. Clodagh smiled a little.

"What's up with you anyway?" Mike asked.

Clodagh watched as a group of girls walked past smiling and laughing, all dressed in brand new uniforms with shiny new shoes and school bags. She recognised them as the dressage girls from Briary. The image of a frightened Ozzie filled her mind for a second and she felt a pang of guilt. She was here and he was still stuck in that awful place. The boy she'd seen on him wandered up to and fell in step next to the girls. He seemed a little younger and keen to impress them.

"Erg, did you see the nag that the school had me on yesterday? It's clearly dangerous, Mother is insisting they sell it."

The girls looked unimpressed, but one nodded at him with a fake smile. The bell rang loudly.

"I'll tell you later," Clodagh said as she stepped into the classroom.

Math's was her second least favourite lesson after P.E. Fitting then that it should start off the new term. Clodagh sat by the window glancing out at the fields beyond the schoolyard. Her mind flicked between hoping Ozzie was at least out in one of the fields safe for the moment and replaying the lesson in her head over and over. Sometimes she imagined she managed to stop it, that she saved him, but that daydream fell flat very quickly. It felt like the longest class ever.

"So, what? The riding school can get away with just beating a pony?" Mike asked.

He sat next to Clodagh on the low stone wall that ran around part of the schoolyard leaning back with his arms on the grass. Clodagh put her elbows on her knees and rested her chin in her hands.

"He belongs to them," she said.

"Yeah, but isn't there like some sort of rules to stop it. I mean like the RSPCA or something," he said. Mike didn't know anything about horses and he wasn't particularly interested in them much either. But he liked animals and hated the thought of any of them being hurt or mistreated.

"He's not being neglected, just treated roughly. It doesn't count, I checked."

Mike sat in silence next to her, but the fact that he was trying to help made her feel a little better, at least someone else cared. The bell rang for class and they stood up heading back into school. One of the other boys in their class deliberately tripped Mike as he went past almost sending him flying.

"Didn't have a growth spurt over the break then shortstop," the boy joked to his friends.

"Bite me, Miles," Mike called back. Clodagh wrapped her arm through Mike's pulling him towards the door. They really were in purgatory, but at least they were there together. As they stepped inside, they passed the Briary girls again, this time one noticed her. She whispered to her friend and they all started giggling.

"What was that?" Mike asked.

"Remember the snotty dressage girls?" Clodagh said. Mike raised an eyebrow and glanced over his shoulder at the girls. Mike whistled, Clodagh nodded.

"They're worse than Miles." He shrugged.

For the next few days, they both seemed lost in thought, but every suggestion they came up with to help Ozzie just wouldn't work. Even Eve noticed they seemed preoccupied, though she never really asked why. There was no way it seemed to save Ozzie and Clodagh began to feel worse than ever. On her walk to and from school, she sometimes caught a glimpse of him in one of the stables or the paddock, but he was too far away to get up to. Somehow those days were harder.

One evening as she was headed home with Sam she saw him alone in the paddock. She stopped and climbed on the fence, leaning over as far as she could just to get a view. He saw her and shouted. Her heart ached. He knew it was her, he knew and was asking her to come to see him, to help him. Clodagh began to cry thinking that he wouldn't understand why she wasn't there, why he'd been taken away. Did the nice girl not want him? Tears began to stream down her face and she couldn't stop them. Suddenly all the frustration started to pour out. Sam caught her arm and helped her down off the fence.

"You should just try to forget the pony. It'll be easier," he said.

Clodagh knew he meant well, knew he was trying in his own way to help, but she suddenly felt so angry and upset she couldn't hold it in anymore. She wanted people to feel as hurt as she did just so maybe they'd understand.

"He's not part of one of your video stupid games," she suddenly yelled, throwing down her school bag. Sam seemed surprised. "He's real and he's my friend and he's scared!"

She ran. Ran full speed leaving Sam behind. Her tears blinded her and she stumbled, picking herself up and running again. She barely paused for the road before she was running again. Her chest burned but she didn't care. She needed to be away. Away from the pain and the hurt and the constant thoughts of Ozzie in that awful place. She dashed through the trees by the paddock only vaguely aware of Sam calling after her and waving her school bag. Mud splashed up her tights but she didn't care. She ploughed on, deep into the woods until she couldn't run anymore and she lent against the rough bark of an old oak tree and sobbed until she couldn't cry anymore.

Pulling herself together she walked up to the manor, not wanting to face anyone at home. She slipped through the rhododendrons and headed down to the ha-ha ditch. The ha-ha bordered the garden too and the stone top was an inviting seat. Clodagh sat down staring out over the paddocks. The place Ozzie had grazed, the incline they cantered up now empty and desolate. Clodagh sniffed.

A wet, cold nose pushed at her hand. Clodagh reached out expecting to find Basil with Ma a few steps behind, but the head she patted was too small. Looking over she saw Pip sitting next to her, his tail wagging, head tilted, ear cocked. Clearly, he knew the small girl was in distress and required dog assistance, but he wasn't sure why.

"Shouldn't you be doing homework rather than sitting on my garden wall?" Mrs. Fitz asked, walking over to her.

Clodagh sniffed and wiped her nose. "Sorry Mrs. Fitz, er Fitzgerald."

"Whatever is the matter?" The old lady asked, leaning on her stick and looking down at Clodagh. She could only imagine how she looked. Mud splattered, tear-stained, tangled hair and probably red-rimmed eyes. There was no easy way out, she could lie to Mrs. Fitz, but she didn't have the energy.

Clodagh took a deep breath and began to tell her everything. How she had taken care of Ozzie like she had been asked, brushed him, talked to him, become his friend. How they had ridden together. She even told her about how different the manor had looked, like it had in the old picture. Mrs. Fitz had smiled at that, a distant look flitting into her eyes as if she could see it too. It had been magic Clodagh said, real magic. Then the nightmare. How she had woken up to Ozzie screaming and been taken away, how she said goodbye through the slats in the cattle truck. Silent tears began to fall again and her voice cracked.

She swallowed hard and Mrs. Fitz waited silently for her to go on. She told the old lady how he'd gone to Briary and Mrs. Fitz squinted her eyes a little, tapping her black cane on the ground.

"Used to be an awful place," she muttered. "Always had a bad reputation in the past, but I was told it was different now. Old owner's daughter took it over, sold their own fields to do it."

Clodagh shook her head, barely taking in what Mrs. Fitz had said. "It's still awful. I went. Aunt Lisa paid for me to go have a lesson and check on him but it was, it was..." Clodagh swallowed back her tears. "There was a boy riding him and he yanked the reins and booted him. Then he fell off and he was shouting and yelling and the instructor, the instructor didn't spot it, she just hit Ozzie and it wasn't his fault, it wasn't. I don't think the saddle fitted and I think it hurt him."

Clodagh let out a sob and blinked hard, twisting her mouth and biting back tears. Mrs. Fitz leant down close to Clodagh, a stern but understanding expression on her face.

"When I was a young girl, our groom quit and my father hired someone else to look after our horses while he was still away with work. The man he hired was an awful lout, loud and brash and fond of taking a whip to the horses. I saw him do it and demanded he stop. Do you know what he said to me?" Mrs. Fitz asked. Clodagh shook her head. "The only way you can make sure your horses are taken care of exactly as you like is to do it yourself. I expect that was his way of saying I should get off my privileged behind and do some work."

"What happened to him?" Clodagh asked.

Mrs. Fitz smiled coldly. "I fired him and took care of the horses myself until my father came home. They were mine after all and if a horse is yours, you decide how they are treated. Sadly, if they belong to someone else that is up to them."

Clodagh sniffed a little. "Thank you."

"You are more than welcome dear. If you need to come sit in the rhododendrons and cry you do so." And with that, she turned around and headed back to the manor.

Clodagh stood up and headed down the drive back home. It was almost dark when she reached the door. As she closed the porch she could hear her Ma on the phone thanking someone and saying yes she's just back now. Clodagh could only guess it was Mrs. Fitz on the phone.

"Just look at the state of you." Ma said when she came in, but through the anger, Clodagh could see how worried she had been. "You best go up and get that filthy uniform off."

Clodagh nodded and went upstairs. Pulling off her tights she glanced over at Tilly box standing on her bookshelf. She wondered if it was big enough. After pulling on her pyjamas and thick dressing gown to help her warm through, she padded downstairs. Ma was in the kitchen making tea. Clodagh picked up the cordless phone from the hall table and slipped into the lounge, glad to find for once Sam wasn't playing a game in there. She sat on the couch, tucking her feet under her and dialing Aunt Lisa's number.

"Hello?" Aunt Lisa said.

"Hi," Clodagh said.

"Hi, how's it going?" Lisa asked.

Clodagh knew Dad had already told her everything about the lesson. She took a deep breath. "I have a plan to help Ozzie."

"Really?" Aunt Lisa said.

"Yeah, I'm going to buy him." There was a pause on the line.

"Clodagh," Aunt Lisa began.

"No, hear me out. I'm going to get a Saturday job and save up. I can try keeping his spirits up as I go and then I'm going to offer to buy him."

"Ok," Aunt Lisa said. "But are you sure they'll sell?"

"Pretty sure," Clodagh said, thinking back to the boy in the corridor.

"You'll have to find somewhere to keep him."

"I know," Clodagh said. "I'm going to start looking once I have some money saved up."

"Well, you certainly seem to have thought it through. I'll help you if I can Clodagh, as long as you talk to your Ma and Dad about it."

"I will. Thanks, Aunt Lisa." Clodagh smiled. She suddenly felt tired as if a weight had been lifted. She had a plan.

Chapter 8

Clodagh pushed open the wooden door hearing the shop bell ring as she did so. She stepped inside looking around the farm shop. Trays full of fresh veg ran around two of the walls and were piled high on tables made out of huge rope reels in the centre, every one full of fresh seasonal veg from the farm. In the summer Clodagh loved the bright colours, things were a little muted now, but there were still lots of different things, carrots, kale, garlic bulbs. Clodagh breathed in the scent of the fresh produce tinged with that of herbs and flowers. Clodagh's eyes landed on some large, red apples. Ozzie would love them; she would have to buy one before she left. On the far wall was a big wooden shelving unit, each of its cube shaped sections full of handmade soaps, candles and lavender bags. She wandered over to it. This was always her favourite part of the shop. In fact, she always found something for Aunt Lisa and Ma's birthdays and Christmas from that section of the shop. Her favourite things were the beeswax candles that came in different colours and scents. She reached out and picked up a pale pink one, sniffing the rose scent. It made her think of summer and sunshine even when she knew there was a thick heavy frost outside.

"Good morning young Clodagh," a cheerful voice said.

Clodagh turned around with a smile as farmer Bob stepped out from the back of the shop. He had his usual flat cap on his head and somewhere beneath his bushy dark beard Clodagh could tell he was smiling.

"Morning farmer Bob," she said.

"What can I do for you today, your Ma need more veg?" Clodagh shook her head.

"Actually, well, I was kind of wondering if you still needed someone to help in the shop," she said a little nervously. Farmer Bob had been saying he needed a Saturday helper for months but no one ever seemed to appear.

"I do as it happens. Why do you know someone?"

"Me?" Clodagh replied, squinting a little as if she feared his answer. "I could do with some money."

Bob stepped around the counter and looked a little worried. "Is everything alright?"

"Yes, well no." She replied honestly, her mind flitting to Ozzie.

"Cup of cocoa?" he asked. Clodagh nodded her head eagerly. Bob made the best cocoa. He sold it every winter festival and Clodagh could never get enough.

Bob pulled up a couple of chairs and Clodagh sat down hovering over her steaming mug, smelling the sweet chocolaty smell. She noticed he'd put in a few extra marshmallows and smiled. He sat down opposite her taking a sip out of his own mug.

"Now then, what's all this about?"

Clodagh began to explain about Ozzie in between taking sips of her cocoa. Now she had a plan to save him. She managed to tell the story without crying which made her feel much better. Farmer Bob sat quietly listening to her tale, occasionally asking questions or saying 'I see' and 'I never'. Finally, she got to her plan and explained about wanting to save up money for him.

"And I remembered you needed some help in the shop. I'd work hard," she said.

"Oh, I've no doubt about that." Bob said. "I know how much you do for your Ma. You think she can spare you?"

Clodagh nodded. "I talked to them about it and Ma and Dad said it was ok. Actually, Dad said he'd be happier if I worked here than somewhere he didn't know."

Bob nodded his head slowly. "Well in that case then." Clodagh looked up hopefully. "You're hired."

A broad smile spread over her face. "Thank you!"

"Trial run mind." Bob added and she nodded. "Weekends we open 10 until 2 and one week night, let's see you finish school at 3.00 yes?" Clodagh nodded. "Let's say 3.30 til 5, and if the shop is quiet you can do your homework, agreed."

"Yes, yes," she said.

"Might have the odd bit of overtime too if you want." Bob added. "Bit hard to be here when I'm busy on the farm." Clodagh nodded.

"Well then, I'll see you Saturday, I'll show you how to work the till. It's not too hard. We serve the customers, sweep up a bit and keep the veg boxes full."

"I can do that." Clodagh smiled.

"Off you go then, best be getting to school." Clodagh stood up putting her mug down on the counter.

"Thanks Farmer Bob."

She was almost at the door when she stopped. She fished out a few coins from her pocket and grabbed one of the shiny red apples and walked back to the counter.

"For Ozzie," she said putting the coins down. Bob pushed the coins back to her.

"You take it. Sounds like that pony needs a treat." Clodagh smiled and thanked him again, picking up the apple and pushing it into her coat pocket.

Ozzie was in the big field by the track when she headed down to school. He was grazing with the little bay pony she'd met at the riding school but as soon as he saw her, he lifted his head, whinnied and trotted over to the fence line. She smiled and started to pat him and scratch his neck. She realised how much she had missed just being with him. Sure, she loved to ride him, but she loved grooming him and petting him too. She gave him the apple and he ate it readily. Clodagh couldn't help but notice his coat wasn't quite as shiny as it had been when she was grooming him. It almost looked dull even though there were no patches of mud on him. She lent over the fence and stroked his back. She could feel how tense it was where the saddle had been. He twitched a little when she ran her fingers over it and his ears flicked back for a second. It was obviously sore; how did they not see it? Clodagh looked over him closely. He looked like he'd lost weight too close up. His coat was quite thick so unless you felt him, he looked alright, but as soon as her hand ran over his side she could tell he was thinner.

"Oh Ozzie," she sighed. "I'm working getting you out, I promise I am."

She rubbed his head and put her forehead on his own holding him close. "Hang in there my friend." He snorted a little.

For a few moments they stood there together just enjoying each other's company before she had to head to school. Leaving him in the field was hard. She struggled to go, especially when he followed her to the corner of the field and stayed stood there as she followed the trail down to the main footpath, but she knew she had a plan now. She wasn't going to let him down. She looked back over her shoulder silently promising him she'd be back and hoping he understood.

She found Mike waiting for her by the gate. He was trying to undo a knot in his rucksack straps. She raised an eyebrow questioningly at him.

"Miles?" she asked.

"David." He replied. "Because my older brother is a jerk who thinks this is funny." Clodagh smiled sadly and helped him untie his bag straps. "Thanks. How come you're late?"

"I went to see farmer Bob."

"And?"

"And I am his new shop assistant," she smiled. Mike nodded his approval and they headed into school together.

"So, if we have an Ozzie plan sorted, you think you could help me come up with a way to get back at David?" he asked. They laughed and for the first time in ages Clodagh felt hopeful. Ozzie wasn't safe yet, but at least she was working on it.

The next few weeks went by in a blur for Clodagh. She settled into work at the shop very easily. She'd grown up with clients coming and going at the B&B and the shop customers weren't that different. In fact in most cases she knew them so it was easier. It was actually nice to talk to the people who came in and for the first time Clodagh could understand why Ma liked what she did. Bob was a great boss. He taught her how to use the till and she even helped him alter the shop layout a little to make more of the homemade candles and soaps he had. He promised as soon as winter fair started up he was going to put her in charge of cocoa and gave her his special recipe which made her feel very proud indeed.

Whenever she had the chance, she took overtime and worked as hard as she could. She swept the shop and tidied up whenever there were no customers. Ma even took her to the bank in town and set her up a proper bank account to put her wages in too, which was amazing and made her feel very grown up. School wasn't any worse, or any better, but at least she and Mike kept each other company.

He even came to the shop after school a few times when she would have been on her own to keep her company. They spent the time quizzing each other for varying tests in between serving customers.

Ozzie wasn't as lucky. Clodagh spent as much time as she could with him, visiting with him when he was in the paddock and sneaking him apples and carrots when she could. Farmer Bob even put a sack in the back room he filled with any stock that was bruised or maybe a little too old to sell just for him, but he was still losing weight. Sometimes she crept down to the school on Sundays to watch the lessons, but more often than not she wished she hadn't.

The instructor was always yelling and the kids seemed not to understand that Ozzie was real. It was as if they thought he was a bike or something that had no feelings. It made her so upset Ma stopped her from going down to spy on him unless he was in the paddock. She was clearly unhappy with the way he was treated though. Clodagh caught her advising a guest against going there for a lesson once and she didn't mince words as to why.

She'd been working at the shop for just over a month when the instructor from the school turned up at the B&B. Clodagh almost didn't recognise her when she rang the bell and Sam answered. Seeing who it was, Clodagh quickly hid behind the coat stand so she could find out what was going on. For a second, she was worried it was about Ozzie or maybe what had happened at the school, but it was clear that the woman had no idea who Ma was.

"Oh, hi, you run the B&B?" she asked. Ma nodded her head and crossed her arms over her chest, her lips pursed slightly. Clearly Ma recognised her. The instructor seemed oblivious to Ma's irritation. "Well, I'm from the riding school down the road. We were wondering if we could leave some leaflets? Sort of local businesses helping one another."

"I'm not exactly sure our clients would be interested." Ma said in her 'I'm saying no politely' voice.'

"I'm sure some might," the woman said brightly. "Who doesn't like ponies?"

Ma looked angry, angrier than Clodagh had expected. "I'm sorry, I won't advertise somewhere that treats animals like you do," she said and promptly slammed the door in the shocked woman's face.

Ma walked away from the door muttering about who the heck the woman thought she was and lamenting that the sprinkler wasn't plugged in. Clodagh stifled a giggle, but as soon as she stepped out into the hallway and caught Sam's shocked expression, they both burst out laughing. Point one for Ozzie.

"Ma sure told her," Sam said.

"Yeah," Clodagh replied, then she frowned. "But I wonder why she's advertising? She's never been here before."

"Who knows," Sam shrugged. "Who cares?"

Me, Clodagh thought, if it affects Ozzie. She decided she needed to keep an extra close eye on him from then on. Surprisingly though everything seemed normal. Bob set up the winter fair at the farm, selling Christmas trees, cocoa and handmade decorations. Ma got the Christmas decorations out; Dad chose a tree from the woods for both the B&B and the manor and Clodagh checked on Ozzie frequently. Other than looking duller and thinner, he was still Ozzie. In fact, Clodagh almost forgot about the instructor coming by with the leaflets until one morning just before Christmas when Sam came in holding the local newspaper with a frown on his face.

Chapter 9

The local newspaper paper landed on the chunky kitchen table with a thud and Sam slid into his chair pushing it across to Clodagh. He tapped the page with a finger and she glanced up from her porridge looking at him with a quizzical expression. He never read the paper and she only ever flicked through the what's on section during the holidays.

"Is that the riding school you keep banging on about? The one with the snotty instructor Ma chased the other day?" he asked.

Clodagh noticed Dad throw a side-long glance at Ma who suddenly became more focused on the pan she was scrubbing in the sink. Clodagh pulled the paper closer, turning it around so she could read the article Sam was pointing at. There in bold print were the words 'Local Riding School to Close' with a picture of the snotty instructor standing smiling beside a horse, her hand wrapped around its nose as if she were hugging it. An image of her slapping Ozzie in the face flashed through her mind, making her feel angry. Clodagh snatched the paper up, all thoughts of breakfast forgotten. She pushed her bowl aside so she could spread out the paper and read it more carefully. Both Ma and Dad appeared behind her, reading over her shoulder and even Sam seemed interested.

The article painted the riding school as a pillar of the community that helped children and was devoted to caring for its horses and ponies. It made Clodagh feel a little ill. She almost felt like storming down to the paper's office and telling the writer what it was really like. Ma must have felt the same as she occasionally muttered 'really' somewhat sarcastically, 'it didn't look like that to me' and even 'the lying toerag' all of which seemed to make Dad raise an eyebrow. The article focused on how the poor owners were facing financial hardship with rising insurance costs and increased rent. Dad started muttering when he read about the rent, something along the lines of 'Mrs. Fitz didn't mention she put the field rent up?' Clodagh wondered if it was an embellishment made by the paper to add drama or if Mrs. Fitz really did put up the rent? The manor did seem to need some extra income and putting the rent up made sense. Then there was the fact Mrs. Fitz hadn't seemed at all happy about the riding school when Clodagh had told what it was really like. Had the old Lady put it up to stop them being cruel to the horses? Clodagh thought back to her story about the groom, she certainly wouldn't put it past Mrs. Fitz after hearing that tale.

Her attention went back to the article and she read on. There was a whole section about the owner, who seemed to be the snotty lady, Clair, trying to find somewhere else to set up. She apparently had 'a few locations close by in mind'. Clodagh started to worry. Did that mean she was going to move Ozzie away! It was bad enough with him at Briary but close enough for her to see him and try to keep his spirit alive. She read on her heart racing and then she read something that made her heart leap with joy. There it was printed in black and white, *several of the larger horses have already been loaned out to Clair's clients. All of the remaining riding school ponies, tack, and some equipment will be sold at auction after the holidays. Clair hopes to use the funds raised to help her set up again in the near future.*

Clodagh couldn't believe it. She read and re-read the article letting the words sink in. Ozzie was going to be sold. She didn't need to go and deal with Clair, didn't need to haggle or anything, didn't have to live with the idea that they might not sell him to her. All she had to do was take her money and buy him. A smile spread across her face. She looked up at Ma, her blue eyes shining. Ma smiled back and winked at her before going back to the dishes. Dad was still staring at the paper wondering when Mrs. Fitz had put up the rent. Unable to take it anymore she jumped up out of her chair, Basil leapt up to her in enthusiasm and she caught his paws almost dancing with him around the kitchen, his tongue lolled out of the side in a lopsided doggy grin. The girl pack member was happy so he was happy. Ma started to laugh, though Dad still looked confused.

"Why are you so happy?" Dad asked.

"She has a chance to get her pony," Ma pointed out. "Ozzie, she can buy him from the auction without dealing with that dreadful Clair woman." Dad raised an eyebrow at her again.

"Where is she going to put it?" Sam asked, looking up from his seat at the table as he shoveled a spoon full of Cheerios into his mouth.

Clodagh stopped dancing suddenly. Sam was right. She lowered Basil's paws down and grabbed the paper again scanning the article. It simply said 'after the holidays', when after the holidays? How long did she have to find somewhere? She looked suddenly around, panicked.

"Don't worry," Dad said, knowing immediately what she was thinking. "You've got at least a month to find somewhere. A sale like that will be at the mart in town and it isn't open again until mid-January. They'll print the listings a fortnight before."

"Print the listings?" Clodagh asked, confused.

"Sure," Dad said, pouring himself a coffee from the pot. "The mart will print a list of every item or animal in this case, being sold. They'll be given a lot number and a reserve price."

"Reserve price?" Clodagh asked, suddenly realising she didn't know anything about auctions. She felt her throat going dry. Suddenly she was starting to feel worried again. One moment it was easy, she would buy Ozzie everything done. Now she was thinking about where he'd live and if she had enough money to get him in the first place.

"Don't worry love," Ma said. "Nothing you can do before Christmas really. Try and enjoy the holidays, you love this time of year. Besides you might get money for Christmas you can add to your wages and farmer Bob said he had extra hours for you at the winter festival over the break."

Clodagh smiled. Ma was right, she had to focus on the positive, keep hope. She decided to carry on with her plan and to try and find somewhere for Ozzie to go if, no when, she bought him at the auction.

"Best get going," Ma said to her and she glanced at the old black wrought iron clock on the wall. Work, she'd be late if she didn't hurry. Grabbing another mouthful of her slightly warmed apple juice, she kissed Ma and Dad, patted Basil, waved at Sam, and rushed to get her coat and boots.

It was cold outside. The paddock had been dusted white with frost and the puddles had frozen to mini skating rinks. Even the brown leaves had white tinges to their sides, but Clodagh barely noticed any of it. All the way to work all she kept thinking about was Ozzie and the sale. Would she have enough money saved to buy him? No, she would have enough. She had to have enough. Where could she keep him? Maybe Mrs. Fitz would let her use the paddock? No, if she put the rent up for the riding school, she probably needed the money and Clodagh wouldn't have the money to rent the space if that snotty lady Clair didn't. She wished Aunt Lisa lived closer, then she could have kept Ozzie at hers with Matilda. For a second, she imagined what it would be like to hack around on Ozzie with Aunt Lisa on Matilda. She sighed, scuffing up a few frost leaves. She couldn't afford to daydream - she needed a plan.

She was halfway to the farm when the idea struck her. Farmer Bob. He had lots of fields around the farm. Maybe he could take Ozzie, even just for a little while until she could find somewhere else. The thought made her feel happy again and she almost skipped the rest of the way to work. She was sure farmer Bob would help her if he could. It was just the sort of person he was. Clodagh decided to ask him as soon as she possibly could.

Bob wasn't at the shop when she arrived. It was the busiest week for the winter fest. The whole front of the farm shop had been decorated with boughs of real holly and ivy with big red bows tied onto them. There were fantastic wreaths laid on tables outside each decorated with different Christmas colours, one even hung on the shop door. Ma had bought one in red and gold with holly and pine cones for the B&B. The guests really loved it when they bigged up the decorations, but she loved it too. Farmer Bob was busy sorting out the Christmas tree lot while Mrs. White who worked in the store most days when Clodagh was at school manned the shop. Clodagh dropped off her bag in the back room. She noticed the pan of hot cocoa had already been set away to bring the hot sweet drink to a simmer and Mrs. White had set out the thermos jug and cups already so Clodagh headed outside to set up the hot cocoa stand. The little stall with its candy cane colours sat just by the shop door, Clodagh hung the open sign out and dusted the frost off the top before she put the mugs in place and set out a sign with the prices on it, before heading inside to pick up the cocoa, marshmallows, and cookies they sold. Mrs. White bustled in and filled the jug for her quickly with a smile as Clodagh picked up her money tin.

"Going to be a busy day dear, but it's awfully cold. You remember to take a break and warm through in the back if you need to," she said and then rushed back into the shop seeing several people come in.

"Thanks," Clodagh called after her. She headed back outside, putting the jug down and unlocking the tin.

She tried not to think about Ozzie, or the field or finding Bob to ask him about both, but it was hard. She focused on smiling and chatting to the customers, pouring them their hot chocolate, and directing them to the tree lot or to the decorations she knew were to be found inside the shop. It was busy which helped, but as the hours passed by, she felt more and more anxious to talk to Bob.

Clodagh was beginning to think she would never get a chance to ask about Ozzie when Bob finally came wandering over to the stall.

He looked tired but still managed to smile at her. He clapped his hands together trying to warm up his fingers.

"Oh, pour me a cup eh Clodagh. I need a pick me up. I don't think I've ever sold so many trees before." He lent on the stall and mopped his brow and smiled, as she poured him a cup popping in the marshmallows.

"Has Dad been by yet?" she asked not wanting to ask about Ozzie straight away, somehow it didn't seem polite. Dad had promised to come and get the hall tree today. She wondered if maybe he had been there already and if he'd mentioned the auction.

"Not yet. Is he coming for a tree?"

"Just the one for the B&B hallway, he gets the living room one for us from the manor woods," Clodagh said honestly.

"Got a really nice 5ft one, would fit perfectly in the hallway I should think, I'll put it to one side for him."

Clodagh smiled. "Thanks. Em, farmer Bob?"

"Yes?"

Clodagh swallowed; this was it. "Did you hear the riding school is closing? They're going to auction off the horses."

"Well," said Bob sitting down on a log by the stall. "Ain't that something. That should give you a good chance of getting your pony, eh?"

Clodagh nodded. "I was wondering if maybe you had a field or a paddock, I could put him in. Not forever, just, I'm trying to find somewhere to take him to if I get him, when I get him," she corrected herself.

Farmer Bob looked at her sadly. He glanced down at his lap for a second. "I'm sorry Clodagh. You know I'd help you if I could, I really would, but all of my land's been ploughed and planted already. Only grass at mine is the lawn."

Clodagh sighed. She hadn't thought about that. "Well, if you know of anywhere..."

"You'll be the first to know," he said, tapping his knee with his cap as he stood up before pulling it on his head. He turned to head back to the tree lot but paused and turned back.

"Tell you what, I have to go to the feed store in town next week. I'll ask around while I'm there."

Clodagh smiled. "Thanks."

He wandered away back to the tree lot. Several customers walked up and distracted her with orders for cocoa. It helped to stop her thoughts from muddling into a mess, at least for a while. She couldn't help but feel disappointed. She had hoped that after talking to farmer Bob everything would have been sorted, now she was back at square one.

It was a long day. Dad came by late in the afternoon to pick up the tree in the old manor flatbed truck. He offered to wait for her to finish up and drive her home but she wanted to walk. Maybe it would clear her head. She didn't want to feel dejected after her plan to take Ozzie to the farm had fallen flat, but she did. She had let herself imagine farmer Bob welcoming Ozzie to some field near the shop so she could check on him in her breaks. How had she not thought about the fact they were ploughed and ready for crops?

She found herself thinking about all the local fields, who owned them, and if Ozzie would be welcome. The problem was the more she thought about it the fewer options she found. There were some farms close by but she had no idea who owned them and others she knew but weren't suitable. She couldn't keep him too far away either, Ma and Dad were too busy to be driving her around, not to mention the cost of fuel.

Clodagh wandered along the edge of the paddock opposite the house. She absently began to kick a pine cone along and twirl one of her pigtails, oblivious to the world.

"Why do you look so sullen tonight? And what did that pine cone ever do to you?" Mrs. Fitz's voice cut through Clodagh's thoughts.

She looked up to see the old lady standing by the fence leaning on her black cane. Pip was running around the paddock with a tennis ball, rushing back and forth with it and occasionally bringing it to Mrs. Fitz for her to throw. It always amazed Clodagh how much energy the springer spaniel had; Basil never rushed around that fast or that much.

"Sorry, Mrs. Fritzgerald. I, I guess you heard about the riding school closing," Clodagh said.

"Good news for the ponies," Mrs. Fitz replied.

Clodagh nodded. "I hope the loss of the rent won't be too bad."

"No," she said. "In fact, I think I've found someone who might be interested already anyway. And that pony you fell for; he'll hopefully get a better home now."

"Hopefully," Clodagh said with a smile. "Actually, hopefully with me. I want him. I'm going to try and buy him."

Mrs. Fitz turned around regarding her carefully. "Really?"

Clodagh nodded. "After what you said. I decided I was going to save up and offer to buy him from the riding school. I got a job working for Farmer Bob, I mean Mr. O'Connell. I'm going to go to the auction."

"I see," she replied. "So why are you kicking innocent pine cones?"

"Well, I think I can buy Ozzie, but I don't actually have anywhere to keep him. I asked Mr. O'Connell if I could keep him at the farm, but all of the fields are ploughed." She looked down at her feet. They were beginning to feel numb now the temperature was plummeting again. The frost that had melted in the weak winter sun was beginning to form again on some of the old brown leaves covering the ground.

"I don't see why you can't just put him back in the paddock," Mrs. Fitz said. Clodagh looked up, a little stunned. "Probably parch the gateway though if he was in there all year so you'd be best using the whole field, top in the summer, bottom in the winter, or the other way around."

Clodagh stared at Mrs. Fitz, unsure of what to say. "Re, really? You, you would let me keep him here? How much would it cost?"

Mrs. Fitz waved her hand a little. "Oh, I wouldn't charge you. Pony would save your father a job. If the paddocks aren't grazed, he'd have to cut them and I cannot afford to buy a tractor yet," she replied.

"Thank you! Thank you!" Clodagh said smiling. It all felt so surreal. She felt as though a weight had suddenly been lifted from her. Everything was starting to fall into place. She was earning the money she needed to buy Ozzie, there would be an opportunity for her to get him and now she had the perfect place to keep him too. Without even thinking she darted over to Mrs. Fitz and hugged her. The older lady stiffened for a second as if surprised, but then seemed to relax.

"Thank you!" Clodagh said and then she was running, rushing towards home, a huge smile on her face, keen to tell Ma and Dad what had happened, as she did, she thought for just a second, she saw Mrs. Fitz smile, but it was getting dark so she couldn't quite be sure. Suddenly it felt like Christmas might be a good one after all.

She burst through the door calling Ma and Dad. Her mother was stringing garlands down the staircase and Dad was putting the final touches to the hallway tree. It looked magical, the green tree covered with little yellow twinkling lights, big red bows, and golden baubles and the natural garland with the same red ribbons. It was as if Christmas had landed when she was out. Somehow it seemed perfect. She'd just got an early Christmas present and it matched the decorations perfectly.

"You'll never believe it," she said. "I found somewhere for Ozzie!" Dad and Ma exchanged glances.

Clodagh took a sip of hot cocoa and bit into a sweet mince pie. The mug felt good in her hands, warming her fingers. Dad sat opposite her at the far side of the heavy wooden table. He looked as if he couldn't quite believe what he was hearing.

"You hugged her," Sam said, staring at her in disbelief. Clodagh nodded, her cheeks reddening a little.

"And she said you could use the field," Dad said. "For free."

Clodagh nodded.

"Actually," Ma put in, placing some more sandwiches and a cake on the table. "She said he could cut the grass better than you by the sound of it dear."

Dad helped himself to a ham sandwich and began eating it still trying to get his head around what was happening.

"But you hugged her," Sam said. Clodagh smiled and nodded.

Chapter 10

Christmas passed in a blur of fair lights and frosty mornings. Clodagh tried to get down to the fields near Briary as often as she possibly could, even on Christmas day, fetching Ozzie bits of food and keeping his spirits up. The colder weather hadn't helped him keep his weight up and he was starting to look really thin. The other ponies looked like they were in a similar state and she was starting to worry about all of them. She started wondering if there was some way to sneak Ozzie a little more food and often found herself giving a few bits to Ozzie's bay pony friend and to a little black mare that was often stood alone by the gate. Aunt Lisa had been angry when she'd told her about it during a call on Christmas day. She had said the owner should be reported, but since the horses were being sold anyway, they decided not to. She really didn't want to jeopardise her chances of buying him. Aunt Lisa had suggested barley might help Ozzie keep some weight on and Clodagh had wondered if she could buy a bag from the feed store and slip some to him.

Then, one morning shortly before school was due to start, she went to check on Ozzie and noticed that several big round hay bales had appeared in the field. Ozzie was happily scoffing down big lumps of one, though he did trot over to her for his usual carrots and apples. At first, Clodagh thought maybe the riding school had finally started to care that the horses were looking thin and that was why they had put out the hay, but part of her began to wonder why now?

She headed to the farm shop feeling uneasy, but at least happy Ozzie had food and she could save the money she was going to spend on the sack of feed towards buying him instead. It would be so much better when he was back home with her. He wouldn't be hungry or cold or poorly treated. She'd even found herself looking online at rugs to keep him dry in bad weather. Swinging the shop door open to the sound of the familiar bell Clodagh headed straight to the vegetables picking up the items on the list Ma had given her and popping them into paper bags. The familiar figure of farmer Bob appeared in the doorway. He smiled beneath his bushy beard.

"Morning farmer Bob," she called.

"Morning Clodagh. I'm glad you stopped by. I have something for you." He disappeared into the backroom for a moment and reappeared with a thick beige catalogue in his hand. "I was going to call up and drop it off when I closed up, you've saved me a trip."

Clodagh looked at him a little puzzled. She reached out and took the thick brochure from him, unfolding it until she could see it more clearly. There was a large black symbol printed on the front she didn't recognise.

"It's the auction listings for the mart, the riding school ponies are in it," he said. "I was down at the feed merchants this morning when the man from the mart came in to drop them off. Picked one up for myself too, there's some decent farm equipment being sold off."

Clodagh swallowed hard. "Thanks."

Things suddenly fell into place. That was why there was hay in the field. It wasn't because they cared, it was because of the sale. Underfed, unhealthy-looking ponies wouldn't do as well at the auction. Clair was fattening them up a bit before the auction. Clodagh suddenly felt even angrier than she had before.

"No problem," Bob was saying. Clodagh stood staring at the catalogue. "Well, aren't you going to look?"

Clodagh swallowed hard. She wanted to. More than anything she wanted to tear through the pages and find him, but she had to get the things back to Ma. She put the catalogue in her bag, her hands shaking a little as she did.

"I'll wait until I get home." Farmer Bob nodded his understanding. He rang up the few items Clodagh had and she paid before snuggling them in carefully next to the catalogue.

Saying bye to farmer Bob she headed home as quickly as she could. Ma was busy doing the laundry when she got back and Dad was nowhere in sight. She stashed the veg in their usual place and ran as fast as she could to her room, her bag clutched tightly in her hands.

Flopping down on her bed she pulled out the catalogue and stared at the glossy front cover. Her eyes scanned over the logo of the mart at the top. With quivering fingers, she began to open the thick pages. The first few seemed to be given over to farm machinery, tractors, harrows, and balers. Finally, she saw a subsection marked horses and under that the word Briary. This was it. She traced her finger down the line of horses. None of them had names. There was a lot number and a description but nothing else. For a few seconds, she felt she may never find Ozzie. She felt her pulse rate jump, what if he had been one of the ponies loaned? That thought hadn't crossed her mind before and she began to worry. What if the horrible boy loaned him? Or one of those snooty girls! She tried to calm herself down, the boy didn't like him and he was still in the field. Deep breaths, she told herself, he's here somewhere.

She re-read the page. Bay Welsh section D gelding, Chestnut mare, piebald, dun, the list went on, all with heights and breed if there was one, she reached the bottom of the page without seeing a grey gelding at all. She turned the page. There on the top of page 2 were the words Lot 439 Grey Connemara gelding, 14.3hh. Ozzie, it had to be Ozzie, Aunt Lisa had seen the picture of him Sam had taken and suggested he looked like he at least had some 'connie' in him as she put it. Her eyes scanned to the reserve price and she felt her heart freeze. She swallowed, feeling tears beginning to form. There was exactly £250 in her account and maybe five more in Tilly box and yet there, right next to Ozzie's name was the reserve price of £400 mocking her. She pushed the catalogue away letting it slip to the floor with a thump. No, it couldn't be.

She grabbed her pillow pulling it to her chest almost feeling like she couldn't breathe. She was so close. She had saved, she had worked, she had even found somewhere to keep him. It couldn't be over, not like that. It just couldn't. It was like some cruel joke. Clodagh felt panicked and her mind began to whirl. She had to do something, find some way of saving Ozzie. If she didn't get him, who would? Where would he go? He could end up somewhere worse than Briary. She started to imagine him being loaded into a box at the mart, crying and shouting as he had on the driveway. It couldn't happen again. She almost started to cry, then her eyes fell on the Tilly box. Aunt Lisa. Aunt Lisa would know what to do.

Springing up from her bed she snatched up the catalogue. She ran down the stairs to the hallway and grabbed the phone from the hall stand. She could feel the tears trickling down her cheeks even though she refused to sob. She huddled on the couch keying in Aunt Lisa's number. Suddenly she felt cold, even with the wood burner on she was shivering. She pulled the thick woolen blanket off the back of the sofa pulling it over her shoulders trying to warm up. The phone rang and rang, please pick up Clodagh willed, please. Maybe she was out teaching or riding Tilly.

"Hello?" Aunt Lisa sounded a little breathless. Clodagh let out a breath of relief.

"Aunt Lisa! Ozzie, his reserve price, I got the listings and it's more than what I have. What do I do?" she rushed.

"Clodagh?" Aunt Lisa asked. "Calm down honey, what's wrong?"

Clodagh took a deep breath and tried to organise her thoughts. "It's Ozzie. I went to the shop this morning and farmer Bob gave me the catalogue for the sale. Ozzie, his reserve price." Her voice broke a little and she sniffed back her tears. "He's £400! I don't have that much, I just, it's too much! What should I do?"

Clodagh felt tears dropping from her cheeks onto the blanket and she shivered more, pulling the warm wooly rug closer around her and trying to stop her hands shaking.

"How much do you have?" Aunt Lisa asked calmly.

Clodagh swallowed; she took a deep shuddering breath trying to calm herself down. "£250. That's everything I earned and my Christmas money."

"Right," Aunt Lisa said. Clodagh could almost hear her thinking. "I have £100 you can put towards him."

"What? Aunt Lisa, are you sure?" Clodagh said, stunned.

"I'm sure. That pony needs a good home. I would only spend it on a new numnah and things for Tilly and she has plenty. You take it if it'll help you get Ozzie."

"Thank you, thank you!" Clodagh sobbed suddenly feeling a mixture of relief and worry.

"Right, that leaves you fifty pounds to find to make the reserve, and remember someone may bid higher. Could your Ma and Dad help?"

Clodagh swallowed hard. "No, not this soon after Christmas, but I could ask farmer Bob if I could get an advance on my wages, at least the £50 so I have the reserve cost."

"Alright, you talk to Mr. O'Connell, do you think he'll help?"

"Yeah," Clodagh said, suddenly feeling more hopeful. She wiped her tears away with the sleeve of her jumper. "I'm sure farmer Bob would help. I could do some overtime to pay him back quicker."

"Ok," Aunt Lisa said. "I'll send the money to your account right now. Try not to worry Clodagh."

"Thanks Aunt Lisa," Clodagh said again with a sniff.

She hung up the phone and sat for a second watching the flames dance in the wood burner and wiping her eyes. A creak behind her made her turn to look at the door but there was nothing there. She sniffed again and stood up folding the blanket up and putting it back on the sofa glancing at the clock on the wall as she did so. There was still an hour before tea. She could just make it to the shop and back if she ran all the way.

Clodagh slipped out into the hallway and put the phone back on its cradle before pulling on her coat and scarf. Sam came wandering down the staircase, his dark hair flopping as he bounced down the steps.

"Sam, can you tell Ma I've popped out to see farmer Bob? I'll be back as quick as I can," she said still feeling rushed.

"It's getting dark," he pointed out.

"I know." She replied, pulling on her gloves.

"Is this about the pony?" he asked, looking down and hovering his foot over the last step. She looked up at him suddenly, her long blond ponytail flicking as she stood up. He smiled at her, peeking out from behind his floppy dark hair. "Heard you on the phone to Aunt Lisa."

"I'm short on the reserve price. I'm going to ask farmer Bob if I can get an advance," she explained.

Sam stepped off the last step into the hallway. He walked over to her and held out his hand. In it were three £20 notes. He waved them at her.

"Go on, go save the stupid pony," he said.

She stared at his hand in disbelief. He waved it again. Slowly she reached out and took the money, she looked up at him surprised, this time the tears brimming in her eyes were gratitude. She sniffed.

"Are you sure?" she asked. He nodded his head. "Thank you!"

"It's no big deal, I was just going to buy a new video game. You can pay me back later," he said with a shrug.

Clodagh suddenly smiled. She almost launched herself at him pulling him into a hug. He half hugged her back.

"Thank you, really, thank you. I promise I will pay you back, I will."

"Whatever," he said sounding disinterested, but she could see his reflection in the mirror and the smile on his face.

Ozzie was coming home; she just knew it. She had overcome so much it had to be. Clodagh suddenly felt warm again, hope flooding in. Her family had helped her and they'd helped Ozzie, everything was going to work out.

Chapter 11

Clodagh studied the shelf of scented soap in front of her, but her mind was elsewhere. She found herself thinking over the amount of money in her bank and what she would have soon. Thanks to Sam and Aunt Lisa she had the reserve price for Ozzie, but what if someone else bid on him too? She had asked farmer Bob if she could have any money she earned up to the auction the day before rather than waiting until her usual pay day and he had happily agreed. Oddly Mrs White had suddenly decided to take a week's holiday too and farmer Bob had offered her overtime which she had gladly taken. It would definitely help. She'd have a little extra just in case. Would it be enough though? She moved the rose soap around again, not sure if she had moved it back to where it had been before and not really looking at what she was doing.

It had felt like it had taken a frustratingly long time for the auction to come around but now it was the next day she felt as if it had sprung itself on her out of nowhere. She added some more soap from the box in her hand into the basket on the shelf. She wondered if the auction would be busy. It was a Saturday, but then it was January and just after Christmas, farmer Bob had said it could go either way.

Mike swivelled around on the stool next to the shop counter while Clodagh added some Rose candles to the shelf one at a time, her hands working while her head was at the auction. He ran a hand through his hair and stared at the paper in his hand.

"I can't believe we have a test the second week back at school. Who does that? I mean did Mr Peters spend his entire holidays dreaming up ways to torture us?" he said picking up a sheet of paper and tapping it with the back of his hand.

"Don't know," Clodagh replied absently.

Mike rolled his eyes. "Earth to Clodagh?"

"What?" she asked looking back over her shoulder. "Sorry Mike. I'm sort of distracted."

"Really, I could never tell!" He smiled "Thinking about the auction?" He asked. She smiled and nodded.

"Ma and Dad can't go. Ma has guests checking in and Dad has to do something up at the manor."

"Does that mean you can't go?" Mike said, suddenly paying more attention. "Cos you know, if you need someone to go with you..."

Clodagh smiled and stepped off the small ladder she'd been on. "I thought about taking the bus, but farmer Bob is going, he said he'd give me a lift and if I do win, he promised to follow me in the landy as I led Ozzie home."

"So why are you so distracted?" Mike asked.

Clodagh sat down on the ladder thinking. It was a hard question to answer. "I guess I'm a little worried about going without Ma or Dad. I've never been to the mart before. But, I'm more worried about the bidding. What if someone else bids too? I don't have much more than the reserve."

Saying it out loud made Clodagh's heart sink. She felt a knot in her stomach tighten a little. It was her biggest fear. She'd had nightmares where she'd been bidding and no one seemed to see her, then someone else had bid and bid, the price going higher and higher while Ozzie stood staring at her. She shook the dream away with a shiver.

"I need to focus on something else. What are those practise questions again?" she asked, if she was going to distract herself, she may as well do it in a way that helped her keep her grades up. Ma had been very insistent that she could only take on Ozzie so long as her grades didn't suffer.

"Ok, ok, but for the record I think it'll be fine. I mean you've worked so hard and everyone is rooting for you to get Ozzie. And the mart thing, I mean you're not really going alone, farmer Bob will be there and I bet he's been to like a million auctions," Mike said leaning on the counter with a smile.

"You're right." Clodagh stood up and headed back up the ladder rearranging the purple candles on the shelf and sending the scent of lavender drifting into the room.

"So," Mike said. "What is the chemical symbol of iron?"

"Fe," she replied, not looking back.

"And water is made of which molecules?"

"Erm, 2 Hydrogen and 1 Oxygen," Clodagh replied, stacking the lavender soap in the basket next to the candles.

"For a distracted person you know way too much about chemistry," Mike muttered. Clodagh smiled, her back still to him; she was glad Mike had insisted on coming with her to the shop that evening after school. If he hadn't been here she'd have been driving herself crazy by now.

The door opened with a ring and Clodagh turned to see Ma poke her head in through the gap.

"Hi love, Dad and I felt a little bad that we couldn't come with you tomorrow. He's agreed to get takeaway for us all tonight, I'm off to get it. Do you want pizza or fish and chips?" she asked with a smile

Clodagh's face lit up. Takeaway was a real treat. They almost never got it unless it was a birthday or bank holiday. For a moment her thoughts of the auction were lost as she excitedly squealed. "Ooh pizza!"

"I take it Mike will be joining us," Ma said, glancing over at Mike still sat with the chemistry paper clutched in his hand.

"Yes please, thanks Mrs G."

She smiled at them. "Alright, I'll pick you up on the way home, ok? Mike give your Ma a ring and let her know."

"Will do Mrs G."

"Ok, bye Ma," Clodagh said.

The door closed with a jingle and Clodagh sighed. Between Mike and takeaway, she might just make it through the evening without driving herself mad. Whether she'd sleep tonight was another matter, but at least for now she could think about something other than Ozzie and if this time tomorrow he would be hers or heading off somewhere unknown.

*

The sun broke over the field with amazing colour, rays of gold and orange shimmering off the dewy grass. Clodagh thought it was beautiful. She had been awake long before the sun had begun to rise and sat wrapped in a blanket staring out over the empty paddock praying that by this afternoon there would be a grey pony stood in it once again. The trees lining the drive blazed into colour and Clodagh slid off the window seat and stepped over Basil who had been sleeping on the thick blue oval rug on her floor. He lifted his head sleepily as she headed over to her desk. She brushed her blond hair and pulled it back into a ponytail before grabbing some clean clothes and heading downstairs, Basil following lazily behind her.

She could hear Dad moving around in the living room and just knew he was setting the fire away. A clinking noise from the kitchen let her know Ma was already up and sorting out the breakfast things. Clodagh headed into the kitchen sliding into her usual seat at the table. The old green aga was belting out heat making the kitchen feel warm and cosy, Basil sidled up to it sitting in a hot spot yawning. Slowly he slid down on the tiled floor until he was laid flat in front of it ready to doze away again.

"Morning love, how did you sleep?" Ma asked, sliding some hot toast in front of her.

"Not that well," she replied honestly. Ma smiled sympathetically as she passed her some juice.

"What time is Bob picking you up?" she asked.

"9.00. The mart opens at 9.30 and the sale starts at 10.00," Clodagh replied, sipping at the juice.

"Up a bit early then," Ma said.

"I couldn't sleep. I thought maybe I could help you out a bit," she said honestly. Mike had stayed late the night before and had constantly been taking her mind off things, joking around and suggesting games to play, but once he had gone the worries had quickly crept back in. She had laid awake for hours thinking about exactly how much she could go over the reserve. She'd even checked the amount in her account three times and emptied Tilly's box.

"Well, I could do with a bit of help checking everything is in place," Ma said. The chair scraped back as Clodagh stood up to get started. "After breakfast."

Clodagh sat back down looking at her toast. It wasn't appealing at all, if anything she felt a little sick.

"Come on love." Ma said, sitting down next to her with her own hot toast and a cup of steaming tea. "I know you're not hungry, but you should have something. Ozzie needs you on top form."

Clodagh nodded. Ma was right, Ozzie needed her focused and not sat starving. She picked up the toast and began to eat it. Surprisingly it tasted great and she felt better for having it and the warmed apple juice.

"You have everything you need?" Ma asked.

Clodagh patted her bag hung on the chair. It had the catalogue in it with Ozzie's details ringed excessively in black biro. Her money and his headcollar and lead rope just in case. She'd checked it a million times over the past week, always suddenly worried somehow it had unpacked itself. Ma pushed a Tupperware box across the table.

"Just a couple of sandwiches and a bit of apple cake. Pop it in your bag for later eh love. Oh, and here's a little something for Ozzie." Ma put a large red apple on top of the sandwiches.

Clodagh took the box with a smile and pulled the green cloth bag onto her knee. She was glad the shoulder bag was so big. She put the box and apple in, checking yet again that everything was in place. She glanced at the clock. It wasn't even eight o'clock. This was going to be excruciating.

Chapter 12

Farmer Bob's old green Landrover had barely stopped when Clodagh jumped into the passenger seat. He smiled at her and waved to Ma as she buckled her seatbelt. She waved too as he turned the car around, its chunky tyres crunching on the yellow gravel of the drive.

"You ready then?" Bob said with a kind smile. Clodagh nodded, pulling the bag in her lap closer to her. She could feel her heart pounding in her chest as they pulled out of the manor gates. She had to calm herself down. Tucking a loose strand of hair behind her ear she glanced over at farmer Bob.

"Are you looking for anything in particular for the farm?" she asked, trying to focus on anything but Ozzie.

"Oh, I don't know, could do with a new harrow, the old one's fair rusted now, but to be honest I just enjoy going down the mart every now and then. It's a good chance to talk to folk and you can sometimes find things you never knew you needed," he said, glancing at her. "Plus, there's a sandwich van there, does the best bacon butty in the county."

Bob smiled and Clodagh laughed. The rest of the drive to the auction went by quickly, but it was further away than Clodagh had expected. If and when she bought Ozzie it would be a very long walk back home. Still, she didn't mind and she didn't think Ozzie would either, not if it meant going home once and for all.

The auction mart was much bigger and busier than Clodagh had expected. There were rows of cars and four-wheel drives to one side and trailers, horseboxes, and livestock trucks to the other. Farmer Bob pulled in next to a few other big four-wheel drives and hopped out. Clodagh followed, pulling her bag over her shoulder but clutching the strap so hard her fingers turned pale. Bob glanced over at her as she stared around herself.

"Over there," Bob nodded to the boxes and trailers. "That's where the folks selling park up and anyone planning on buying stock usually. Most of the farm machinery is in that field over there." He pointed at a large green field full of various bits of equipment and a few tractors. Most of us, if we buy anything, arrange to come back for it, otherwise the whole place would be full of tractors," he laughed. Clodagh tried to smile but it was overwhelming. There was noise from the livestock, cows bellowing, and a little bleating of sheep. Somewhere a horse whinnied and for a second, she wondered if it was Ozzie, it was hard to tell amid the general hubbub.

"Where are the horses?" Clodagh asked, her voice almost drowned out by the noise of a tractor starting up.

"All the animals are in the barns. They go in sections, looking at the programme they're doing the sheep first, then the horses, then cows. They'll be stalled in that big barn and brought through into the ring by lot. That's when you bid."

Clodagh suddenly felt very small. She'd known the auction was a big place and a busy one, but this was on a different level. Her heartbeat was so fast she was sure Famer Bob would hear it. I can do this, she told herself, can't I? Farmer Bob looked at her kindly.

"Tell you what, I only have a couple of things to look at today and I do like looking in at the animals. What do you say we stick together? First, we'll get ourselves registered, get a couple of paddles. Then you can help me check over the harrows, your young eyes are probably better at spotting any rusty bits anyway and then we'll go check Ozzie is here, make sure he's ok. We'll grab a butty and go in; I can maybe help you with bidding on the pony," he said with a smile.

Clodagh let out a breath she hadn't even known she was holding and smiled broadly with relief. "Thank you. I'd like that a lot. I'm not sure I could do this by myself."

"Right then, off we go." Bob led the way towards the main auction building explaining how the whole process worked as he went. Clodagh was becoming more and more glad Farmer Bob was there the more he spoke. He seemed to know everything about the mart, even its history, which would have been fascinating if she hadn't been so worried. Inside the main building, they joined a short line of people also registering. Up ahead of them she saw a woman in clean blue jodhpurs, her short, thick dark hair held back in a neat ponytail. She shifted a little as if bored. Clodagh stared at the woman. She doubted she was a farmer in her short boots and half chaps. She was there for the horses; Clodagh just knew it. She had known there would be other people interested in the horses, but right then it became real. She tightened her grip on her bag as the woman got a paddle with a number on it and turned to go. She smiled at Clodagh as she passed by and Clodagh randomly thought that at least she looked nice.

She and farmer Bob stepped up to the desk. The man sat behind it looked up at them over his glasses. Bob smiled and began to register them for the sale. The man glanced at Clodagh with surprise when Farmer Bob started giving him her details, but he took them anyway and handed both of them a white paddle with a black number printed on it. Clodagh looked at it, turning it in her hands as she and Farmer Bob walked away. 108. That was the number that could win or lose Ozzie.

Farmer Bob looked all around the harrows in the green field inspecting them all. Clodagh followed, her mind flicking between

Ozzie, the woman in the queue, and what she represented and the general hubbub of the mart.

"This one looks pretty good," Bob said, rubbing his chin through his beard. "What do you think, Clodagh? Should I go for it?"

Clodagh looked at the harrow, she'd seen them before but never quite so up close, it looked rather scary with its chains and spikes. She looked at it closer for rust as Bob had requested. It looked pretty clean to her and she nodded her approval.

"Right then," Bob noted down the lot number in his programme. "Shall we go see if we can find that pony?"

Clodagh nodded emphatically and they headed off to the main building and the stall area. Inside there was a grid of metal pens carefully laid out, each with straw or shavings in it and hay for the animals to eat. Most of them seemed relaxed and happy to eat, especially the sheep and cows, most of whom seemed completely oblivious to everything going on around them. A few of the horses looked less happy. There were more tensed pricked ears and less eating. Clodagh made her way amongst the pens with Bob looking in each. She wanted to shout to Ozzie, call to him to let him know she was there, but over the noise, he probably wouldn't hear her and she might look a little odd. Eventually, she and farmer Bob agreed to split up and walk part of the grid each.

Clodagh walked through the grid scanning every pony for Ozzie. Up ahead she saw the woman from the queue. She was looking over a pen at a little bay pony. Clodagh realised she knew the bay; it was the one from Briary. She looked around hoping that all the riding school ponies were together, but she couldn't spot Ozzie close by. Clodagh walked closer; she could see the woman frowning. The little bay pony was stood with his back to the woman. He looked tense and was ignoring the hay and eyeing the lady. The pony was nice and he'd been friendly with Ozzie, maybe she could help him out.

"He's really nervous," she said.

The woman turned around and smiled at her. Unlike Clair, this woman's smile reached her kindly blue eyes.

"I can tell," she said.

"He came from the riding school. They didn't treat him very well, but he's nice," Clodagh said. She made a little clicking noise and the pony turned around. Seeing Clodagh he brightened, clearly, he remembered Ozzie's friend that brought them carrots. He shuffled over still eyeing the woman and nuzzled at Clodagh's hand hopefully.

The woman nodded. "You didn't ride there?"

"NO!" Clodagh exclaimed. "Sorry, no, I wouldn't ride there. They didn't treat the ponies very well."

The woman smiled and nodded. "You think he'd be alright in a riding school that treats him well?"

Clodagh thought for a second absently scratching the bay's neck. "I think so. I think he wants to be friendly; he just isn't very trusting."

"Thank you," the woman said. She marked him down on her catalogue.

"Do you have a riding school?" Clodagh asked.

"I hope so," the woman replied cryptically and walked off.

"Who was that?" Farmer Bob asked, coming up beside her.

"I don't know," Clodagh replied honestly.

"Come on, I think I found Ozzie," he said.

Clodagh rushed along with Bob past several horses. There, in a corner was Ozzie. Clodagh felt relief flood through her, at least he was here. She almost ran to the pen.

"Ozzie, Ozzie" she called.

He looked around and whinnied. Abandoning his hay, he came over to her and nuzzled into her. She climbed onto the metal gate of the pen and caught his nose up in a hug almost crying with relief. He was here. He was really here. All she had to do was win the bid and he was coming home. Bob stood behind her smiling.

"Sheep are going in now. I think we have about five minutes before we need to go in." Clodagh glanced at him with a smile. "Say, did you know Mrs. Fitzgerald was coming today?"

"Mrs. Fitz? Here?" Clodagh said, confused.

"I'm fair sure it was her I saw," Bob said. Clodagh wondered if she was looking at one of the tractors, that would surprise Dad, but then she shook the thought from her head. Mrs. Fitz would have just sent Dad if that was the case. Ozzie nudged her with his nose and she forgot all about Mrs. Fitz. She dug around in her bag and pulled out the apple Ma had given her. He ate it in two bites and nudged her again.

"Sorry, Ozzie," she said scratching his neck. "I only brought one."

"Great minds," Bob said, pulling a carrot out of his pocket and handing it to Ozzie. Clodagh giggled.

It seemed like seconds before she had to leave Ozzie in his pen and go find a seat. She kept looking back over her shoulder as she walked away, trying to reassure him she wasn't going forever. He stood and watched her go before returning to his hay net.

The crowd gathered in the mart were mostly farmers. Bob seemed to know many of them and there were lots of hellos and mornings. Seeing how worried she was, Bob took the time to find out what the farmers were after that day. Almost all of them said sheep or cows. A couple were looking for ponies. One was after a Shetland and the other a pony for his granddaughter. To her delight Bob talked to him, explaining about Clodagh and Ozzie. The farmer smiled, glanced at her, and shook Bob's hand at the end of their chat. Bob winked at her and then went to their seats.

The horses began to come in one by one. They were led into a sandy ring, walked and trotted around in each direction by a man who worked for the mart, and then the bidding would begin. A few horses came and went before the bay from Briary came in. He trotted around nervously flicking his ears. The bidding began and Clodagh recognised the lady from the queue bid on him and won. She smiled. Next up was another pony from Briary, the pretty black mare she'd seen in the field a few times. It was always on its own, but very friendly when it had been by the fence a few times. Clodagh nudged Bob and nodded at the mare and tilted her head towards his farmer friend with a smile.

"Mel," Bob called, the man looked over and he nodded his head at the black pony. The man smiled and touched his cap before raising his paddle.

He won the mare. Clodagh just knew it had found a good home and the girl would be more than happy. A string of other horses came and went, including several she recognised from the school or the fields. The woman from the queue bid and won at least another four horses and ponies. Clodagh began to pay more attention to her.

"Lot 439," the announcer said.

Clodagh sat up a little straighter. The gates opened and in came the man leading Ozzie. He walked around the ring one way and the other. Trotted and then stood in the middle of the ring. Clodagh fought the urge to jump up waving the paddle.

"Reserve is set at £400. We'll begin bidding there. Do I hear £400?" the announcer said.

Clodagh waved her paddle. The man pointed at her. "I have 400. Can I get 420."

To her horror the woman from the queue bid. Clodagh swallowed hard. This couldn't be happening.

"420, thank you, can I get 440?" Clodagh raised her paddle. Please be enough, please be enough.

The woman raised her paddle. Clodagh felt sick, Ozzie, she couldn't lose Ozzie. She didn't have much more.

"I have 440 will anyone give me 460?"

Clodagh raised her paddle again. The man acknowledged her and then began to speak again asking if anyone would bid more. Clodagh glanced at the woman and frowned. There, next to the woman from the queue was Mrs. Fitz. She was unmistakable in her quilted gilet and tweed skirt, her grey hair in its usual bun. She seemed to be smiling and chatting with the woman and, was it Clodagh's imagination, she looked over and nodded in her direction. The woman lowered her paddle.

"Any further bid on 460? Last chance. Going once, going twice." The man banged his gavel on the desk. "Lot 439 sold to the girl with paddle 108."

Clodagh stood in shock. She won; Ozzie was hers. A smile spread across her face and she began to bounce up and down. Even Famer Bob joined in her celebrations. Then he stopped, taking hold of her arms gently.

"We need to go pay for him." Clodagh nodded and followed as he led the way back to the entrance where someone could take the money from her. It took a little while to sort everything out, but soon enough she was standing holding Ozzie's passport in her hand. He was hers; he was finally hers. She couldn't stop smiling.

"I guess we have a long walk home," Bob said beside her.

"I don't mind," Clodagh said, staring at the green booklet in her hands.

"You're not walking back to Bob's farm, are you?" a voice asked.

Clodagh looked up to see the farmer that had bought the pretty black mare standing nearby. He too held a horse passport in his hand.

"No Mel, no room on my farm for a pony. Clodagh here lives in the gatehouse of the manor. Ozzie's going there," Bob said.

The old man whistled. He pulled his cap off his head and ran a hand through his grey hair before putting the cap back on.

"It's a long walk that is."

"I don't mind, not one bit," Clodagh said.

"Tell you what, I have the farm along from Bob's. I'm going in that direction and I have space in the trailer. I'll give you a lift. My way of saying thank you for recommending that pony, let me see here." He opened the passport and squinted a little at the name. "Rhys's Dancing Dream. I think we'll just call her Dancer, eh?"

Clodagh couldn't believe it. She looked from Bob to Mel with a smile. Farmer Bob nodded almost to say it was alright.

"Thank you, Mr..."

Bob laughed. "White, Mel here is Mrs. White from the shop's husband."

"Wait, this isn't Clodagh from the shop," Mel said.

Bob laughed again so hard he almost began to cry. "Mel, how many Clodagh's do you know around here?"

"It's a fair point," Mel said, joining in laughing.

"Come on, I'll get us all a bacon butty before we go home," Bob said.

Clodagh found herself sitting on the gate of Ozzie's pen eating the best bacon sandwich she had ever had and telling Mel the whole story of Ozzie. They had managed to bring Dancer down to the pen next door and the pair were happy eating next to each other while they chatted. Mel explained that his daughter and her husband had recently divorced and she was moving back to the farm with his granddaughter. The girl was apparently about Clodagh's age and horse-mad like she was. Mel was hoping Dancer would help her through the divorce and the move. It made Clodagh smile to see how much Mel cared about his family and she was happy to see him, petting Dancer and Ozzie, whenever they wandered over.

"Well, shall we get going?" Mel asked.

Clodagh nodded, though she felt a knot in her stomach. Ozzie hadn't exactly been happy to go on the wagon, in fact, his old owner had said he hated it.

"I'm not sure how happy Ozzie will be going on the trailer," she said honestly.

"We'll put Dancer on first, will we," Mel said. "Now mind, the trailer's a bit old so no expecting something posh." Clodagh smiled.

Mel's trailer turned out to be an old blue one with RICE written on it. The ramp was low and wooden. Inside was a bright cream colour and with the front part opened up it looked quite inviting. As she led Ozzie out on his headcollar she saw the lady from the queue loading the bay pony into the back of a large lorry. She was calm and kind to him when he looked nervous and Clodagh felt happy that he was at least going with someone nice.

Dancer went straight into the trailer for Mel with no fuss at all and happily stood munching. Now it was Ozzie's turn. Clodagh looked at him with a smile.

"Time to go home Ozzie." She scratched his neck and headed up the ramp. He paused for a second with one foot on the ramp. Clodagh turned back to him.

"It's ok this time Ozzie. This time you're staying with me," she said calmly. Ozzie snorted and then carefully and slowly picked his way up the ramp into the box next to Dancer. They seemed to acknowledge each other and then began calmly eating. Clodagh smiled.

Good as his word Mel dropped Ozzie off right at the door. Ozzie had quite the welcoming committee. Dad, Ma, Sam, Basil, and even Mrs. Fitz were standing in the driveway as he backed himself off the ramp. He looked around himself happily, his ears pricked. As Mel drove away Clodagh waved before taking Ozzie back to his paddock.

As soon as he was free, he tossed his head and snaked his neck. He trotted around a little and slid into a roll. He rubbed and scratched and rolled until he was more green and brown than grey. Clodagh laughed and shook her head.

"Oh, Ozzie."

He stood up and shook himself before lowering his head and cramming as much grass into his mouth as he could.

"I told you he'd make a good job on the grass," Mrs. Fitz said to Dad as she began to head back towards the manor.

"Thank you," Clodagh said as she passed her.

"You're quite welcome," she replied with a slight smile.

"You best call your Aunt Lisa," Dad called. "She's rang three times already."

Clodagh laughed. "Alright Dad, in a minute."

Later that night as she got herself ready for bed Clodagh couldn't help but keep opening the curtains to look out at the silver-grey shape in the paddock happily grazing in the moonlight. It was almost as if she thought he may disappear, but he didn't. He was hers now and he was going nowhere. Clodagh sank into her bed feeling better than she had ever thought imaginable.

You did it...

Congratulations! You finished this book.

Loved this book? Consider leaving a review! Book reviews are a valuable way for you to help me share this book about Ozzie and Clodagh with the world. If you enjoyed this book, I would love it if you could leave a review online. Ozzie & Clodagh say a big thank you too!

Enjoy the Show Horse, the next book in this series at

www.writtenbyelaine.com

THE
CONNEMARA
ADVENTURE SERIES

THE CORAL COVE SERIES

www.writtenbyelaine.com

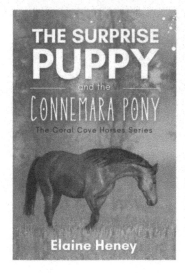

EDUCATIONAL HORSE BOOKS FOR KIDS...

www.writtenbyelaine.com

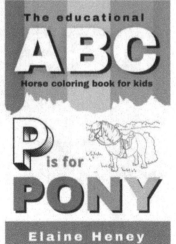

Saddlestone Books

www.elaineheneybooks.com

Made in USA - North Chelmsford, MA
19150_9780955265341
11.08.2023 0832